STRANGER AT THE DOOR

PAULINE SMITH
STRANGER AT THE DOOR

TATE PUBLISHING
AND ENTERPRISES, LLC

Stranger At The Door
Copyright © 2015 by Pauline Smith. All rights reserved.

No part of this publication may be reproduced, stored in a retrieval system or transmitted in any way by any means, electronic, mechanical, photocopy, recording or otherwise without the prior permission of the author except as provided by USA copyright law.

This novel is a work of fiction. Names, descriptions, entities, and incidents included in the story are products of the author's imagination. Any resemblance to actual persons, events, and entities is entirely coincidental.

The opinions expressed by the author are not necessarily those of Tate Publishing, LLC.

Published by Tate Publishing & Enterprises, LLC
127 E. Trade Center Terrace | Mustang, Oklahoma 73064 USA
1.888.361.9473 | www.tatepublishing.com

Tate Publishing is committed to excellence in the publishing industry. The company reflects the philosophy established by the founders, based on Psalm 68:11,
"The Lord gave the word and great was the company of those who published it."

Book design copyright © 2015 by Tate Publishing, LLC. All rights reserved.
Cover design by Joseph Emnace
Interior design by Jake Muelle

Published in the United States of America

ISBN: 978-1-63449-865-4
Fiction / Thrillers / Suspense
14.12.20

To my grandson Jaime, it is my ardent hope that you will continually strive to be the best you can be. May you never be swayed by what is popular, but by what you have been taught by those who love and care about you most. Learn to do for yourself; self-sufficiency is not just for females. Never allow yourself to be led down a path that you know you'll later regret. Always be proud to look yourself in the eye the morning after without shame or regret. Always be aware of those less fortunate than yourself. Help if you can—but do not hurt or hinder at any cost.

To my granddaughter Jasmin, I hope you learn the true meaning of honesty, humility, and integrity. May they be the hallmark of how you live your life. Never let beauty get in the way, but let it shine from the inside out so everyone that comes in contact with its rays will remain forever dazzled. I hope you learn to work for the things you want; you'll appreciate more the unexpected gifts. I hope you learn to make your bed when you wake up each morning; nothing feels better than coming home to a freshly made bed. Bed making is really not overrated.

*Only as high as I reach can I grow, only as far as
I seek can I go, only as deep as I look can I see,
only as much as I dream can I be.*

—Karen Ravn

Prologue

As an only child, Margaret Grant was beautiful as she was charming. She was the most well-behaved baby any mother could ever hope for. Henry and Victoria Grant were second-generation Italians living in East Flatbush. Flatbush was a middle-class residential neighborhood in the borough of Brooklyn, New York. They had given up on having children when to their surprise, Margaret came along when they were in their midforties. They were overjoyed at the new arrival and doted on her from the minute she was born. She had a wonderful disposition, and her parents wished for another child just as perfect as Margaret. However, that wish was never to be granted, and so Margaret grew up an only child. Her one wish at Christmastime was that Santa Claus would bring her a baby brother. However, that was not in the cards.

Margaret was five years old when suddenly their happiness ground to a halt. It started with Henry constantly complaining of a persistent cough and a general feeling of malaise.

"Maybe it's all that dust you're breathing in every day at the factory," Victoria suggested.

"Maybe," replied Henry in between bouts of coughing.

His visit to the family doctor brought unwelcome news. A small shadow was discovered in Henry's right lung, which further tests revealed to be a malignant tumor. Unfortunately, it was far too advanced and inoperable, so the doctor advised him to start getting his affairs in order.

The news was devastating to Victoria as Henry had been her first and only love. They discussed what would happen when the time eventually came.

"I have a brother in Plains," said Henry. "Maybe it's time we pay him a visit and make our peace. We haven't talked in a long time, but I think it's time for us to make our peace." He sighed. "We have no other living relatives, and I want you and Margaret to be okay when I'm no longer around."

Since receiving the news, not a day went by that Victoria did not cry her heart out. *What will I do without him?* she cried. *I've always had him in my life.* And so the plans were set in motion for them to visit and get to know their affluent relatives in Plains, New York.

They had never visited Plains before, so they wanted to allow themselves enough time to find their way. "It's a good distance from here, so I want to take my time," said Henry.

"I agree," replied Victoria.

Traffic on the highway was moving at a steady pace until they entered the Cross Westchester Expressway.

"Oh…traffic is so heavy," said Victoria, looking around nervously. "All these huge tractor trailers, and everyone seems to be moving so fast."

Henry was aware Victoria hated heavy traffic, but there was nothing he could do. He could not turn around on the highway; the best he could do was reassure her. "Just make sure your seat belt is fastened," Henry told her.

He took a quick look back at Margaret all buckled in and asleep in her car seat. No sooner had his eyes left the road than the driver of the semi to his left decided to change lanes. One minute they were driving in the middle lane, and next they were being unceremoniously pushed up against the car in the right lane. The car behind them plowed into their bumper, starting a chain reaction. The driver of the car in the left lane went airborne landing on top of another car, all four wheels spinning in the air. The chain reaction continued with cars unable to stop, all bunching together in a crumbled mass of twisted indistinguishable broken metal.

Henry's car, along with another ten or more cars all bunched together, scaled the divider and started rolling and flipping over each other. The sound of mangled metal filled the morning air accompanied by the acrid smell of smoke from burning rubber. Windshields randomly exploded, and broken glass and debris were scattered all around, some heading directly for Henry's car. As shards of broken glass bombarded her body, Margaret burst into tears. She was thrown clear of the car, landing in a dense clump of grass, still strapped into her car seat. The mass of crushed burning metal continued rolling, bouncing, and crushing everything in its path until finally landing at the bottom of the ravine where it exploded into a massive fireball.

1

Margaret's guardian angel must have been watching over her on that fatal day. She had received only minor scratches and abrasions. However, she remembered overhearing the doctors saying that had it not been for their car's license plate, her parents would have been unrecognizable. The doctors and nurses all said it was a miracle she had survived. She would be going to live with her only living relatives in the suburbs of Plains, New York, as soon as she was better.

She had never met these relatives before. Maybe it was because she had lived with her parents in Brooklyn, and they lived far away in Plains. She did not recall hearing her parents talk about her having a cousin or her father having a brother, and she certainly did not remember visiting with them.

She had only spent a week in the hospital and could remember that a lady and sometimes a man and a little boy had visited her almost daily. Ms. Cooper, the social worker, had brought them to her bedside.

She remembered her introducing them to her. "Margaret, this is your aunt Edith, uncle Albert, and cousin William. You'll be going to live with them when you're feeling better."

They were very nice to her, but still they were not her parents. Aunt Edith had very kind eyes, and seemed to laugh at all of Uncle Albert's jokes. Margaret also laughed at his jokes.

"You're funny," she told him, as she laughed at yet another one of his jokes.

She was happy while they were visiting. She didn't feel lonely, but she couldn't help crying when the time came for them to leave. She felt so all alone.

"I want my mommy and daddy," she cried. The nurses had comforted her the best way they knew how, but she still missed her mommy and daddy.

It seemed like such a long time since she had seen them. The truth was it had only been a week since the accident, but to a five-year-old, it seemed like forever.

The day finally came, and they were here to take her to her new home. She tried to be brave, just like Ms. Cooper, the social worker, had told her, but she still felt sad and alone. That was why she was now hiding behind Ms. Cooper's skirt.

"I'll be coming with you, Margaret, to make sure you're settled in, so don't be afraid," said Ms. Cooper, rubbing Margaret's shoulder affectionately.

She was happy to hear that, so she released Ms. Cooper's skirt and held on tightly to her hand instead while holding on to her doll with the other hand. It was not a very long way from the hospital to her new home, and soon they were getting out of Ms. Cooper's car. Margaret kept looking up at the tall building that was going to be her new home. She thought her neck would hurt from looking up so high. She had never before seen a house this big.

I wonder if they get lost sometimes, she thought to herself.

2

No sooner had they parked and alighted from the car than another boy about William's age came running from the house next door. Her cousin William did the introductions.

"Luke, this is my cousin, Margaret. She's going to live here with us. Luke lives next door," he said, turning and pointing to the house next door.

Margaret stared at him but said nothing, still holding on tightly to her doll. Soon both William and Luke disappeared to do whatever it was that six-year-old boys do. She later realized that the two were inseparable. Wherever you saw one, you could be sure that the other was not far behind.

As she walked into her new home, she tried looking around to see if it was like the house where she used to live with her mommy and daddy.

"This is a nice house," she whispered to Ms. Cooper as she looked on in awe at the high ceilings. Overhearing her comment, her aunt smiled and replied, "Well, thank you, Margaret. I hope you'll like it here."

"Do you like cookies, Margaret?" her aunt asked. "I'm going to bake some in a little while. Would you like to help me?" her aunt asked.

"What kind?" asked Margaret quietly?

"Chocolate chip," replied her aunt.

Margaret nodded her head eagerly and graced her aunt Edith with a shy smile. The thought of warm cookies did the trick, and soon she was busy being her aunt's little helper. Soon the cookies were done and placed on a tray to cool, and before long, she was ensconced on a stool in Aunt Edith's kitchen eating the best cookies she had ever tasted. The cookies were followed by a tall glass of cold milk.

"I think I'm going to like it here," she said softly to her aunt. Her aunt smiled in reply.

Margaret was settling in quite comfortably, so Ms. Cooper decided this was as good a time as any to take her leave. "Margaret, I think I'll be leaving now. I know you'll be very happy here," said Ms. Cooper smilingly. Margaret ran over, and they hugged.

"Good-bye," said Margaret. She and her aunt walked Ms. Cooper to the door and waved good-bye until they could no longer see her car. They then went back inside. "Are you ready for a tour of the house?" asked her aunt.

"Yes, yes," said Margaret, nodding her head excitedly. Her aunt held out her hand, and Margaret took hold of it.

"Would you like to see your room?" her aunt asked. "It's a very nice room. I hope you'll like the toys and books I picked out for you." Margaret nodded yes. "Well, let's start here," said her aunt. They left the kitchen and the mouth-watering smell of chocolate cookies and wandered around for what seemed to Margaret a very long time. First they went to the family room where Aunt Edith told her they all watched television together and played board games sometimes. What made Margaret even happier was when her aunt told her, "This is where we place the Christmas tree and open gifts on Christmas morning."

Next, they visited the living and dining rooms, and finally a room with a lot of books. She marveled at the amount of books in one room. "This is your uncle's library," said her aunt. "If you want to look at a book, you have to first ask him. He does not like anyone removing his books. Do you understand?" Margaret nodded yes.

"I'm afraid I'm going to get lost," said Margaret, looking up at her aunt.

Aunt Edith smiled. "I don't think you will. Just take your time. Get to know a little bit at a time, and in no time, you'll be running around as if you've lived here all your life."

They climbed the stairs to the bedrooms, and Margaret continued to look around in wonder. At the top of the stairs, she asked her aunt, "Do you sleep up here too?"

Aunt Edith nodded. "Yes, I do. Uncle Albert and I stay in that room." She pointed to a door down a long corridor. They continued on and crossed what seemed like a bridge.

"This is going to be your room," said her aunt, opening the door to the most beautiful room Margaret had ever seen. The walls were painted a soft pink with pictures of Cinderella, Snow White, and Tinker Bell all scattered along a border.

"Do you like it?" her aunt asked.

Margaret's eyes opened wide as she stared at the beautiful canopied bed, the pink-and-white bedside lamp, and what seemed like a mountain of new toys. "Yes," she replied, nodding her head vigorously and rushing to get a closer look at the toys.

"If you ever feel afraid, or if you just want to talk, you can always come to my room," said her aunt. Margaret nodded her head again. She reluctantly left all her new toys and followed her aunt down the hallway until they came to the next door.

"This is your cousin William's room," her aunt said, pointing to the door.

The door was closed, so Margaret did not get a chance to see what William's room looked like. *It doesn't matter anyway. I just want to go back and play with my toys*, she thought.

Margaret settled easily into her new home. For a while, she missed her mom and dad, but soon it seemed as if she had lived there all her life. Aunt Edith and Uncle Albert treated her like their own, showering her with love and making sure that she wanted for nothing. The only fly in the ointment was the realization that she was not accepted into William and Luke's so-called boy's club.

"No girls allowed. This club is for boys only," William told her. "You're a baby; we don't want girls in our club," Luke added. As if being a girl was such a bad thing!

They treated her like a little pest, always hiding from her and closing the door to their tree house. Despite all the outward display of intolerance, they were both very protective of her and would never deliberately cause her any harm.

After being constantly snubbed, she realized she had no choice but to find ways of creating adventures of her own. Her spirits were never down for long, and all feelings of exclusion were easily overcome by the love and attention she received from her aunt and uncle.

3

Like William and Margaret, Luke was an only child. He had very good reasons for hanging out at William's house. Not a day would go by that he did not wish that he lived at William's house.

The Stewart household was always full of life, laughter, and the smell of great cooking. Luke enjoyed watching Uncle Albert as he tried to sneak a kiss from Aunt Edith when he thought they were alone. His actions always made her laugh as she would try to slip out of his reach. She would try her best to escape from him but would always allow him to catch up to her. She would then act as if she did not want to be kissed but would always relent and eventually give in.

"Stop it, Albert, you old man," she would say as she playfully slapped his hands while trying her best to cover her smile.

"How do you expect me to behave when I have such a beautiful young bride?" Uncle Albert would respond laughing.

Luke never felt happier than when he saw them hugging or dancing to the oldies on the radio. They never knew that he was watching, but when he returned to his house, before he fell asleep, he would tell himself, "When I'm married, I'll be just as happy as Aunt Edith and Uncle Albert. I want my house to be full of fun and laughter. I want to have lots of kids who will be happy and playful, and I'll play games with my wife…"

He would fall asleep and dream about all the things he observed and enjoyed at William's house. However, he would awake to the disappointment and the reality that it was all just a dream. However, it never stopped him from daydreaming.

Although he had a mother and a father of his own, Luke often wished that the Stewarts were his parents. At his house, there were no sounds of happy laughter, no fun, and most of all no display of affection. No wonder he was always hanging out with William. Despite all the time he spent away from his house, no one ever seemed to miss him. When he returned home, neither his mom nor dad asked if he had had a good day or where he had been. One thing he knew for sure was that while at William's house, he did not have to listen to the sound of voices raised in anger.

4

Eight years later

"Time and tide wait for no man," as the saying goes, and soon eight years had flown by. Luke and William were now in high school and still remained inseparable. It was quite evident, however, to those who knew them, that they were both headed on different paths as far as their future was concerned.

As expected, Margaret did not remain William's pesky little cousin but had now blossomed into a ravishing beauty. At fifteen, she had developed into a beautiful, curvaceous young lady who never failed to turn the heads and get the hormones raging of every teenage male. Her big blue eyes were like limpid pools in which one could easily drown if they focused too long or hard. Her skin was like flawless alabaster. She had the most beautiful smile, which seemed to light up any room she entered. This change was not totally lost on Luke Foster. He couldn't keep his eyes off her, and unbeknown to him, Margaret had also started to develop the biggest secret crush on him.

The prom was not far off, and all the seniors were excited about who they would be taking as their date. The subject came up on one of Luke's regular visits to William's house. They were playing video games in William's room when Luke decided to broach the subject. He paused the game, looked at William, and asked, "So who are you taking to the prom?"

"Well, I haven't asked anyone yet, but I'd love to take Sarah," William replied. "She's Margaret's best friend, but I'm nervous about asking her. Who are you taking?"

"I'd like to take Margaret," said Luke, looking steadfastly at William, trying to gauge his response. He knew that William had become extremely protective of Margaret, and if he was going to get a chance to date her, he would first have to get William's approval. William did not reply, neither did he make eye contact with Luke. "So can you ask her for me?" Luke asked nervously.

William finally looked him in the eye with a look that said "That's my little cousin, and you'd better not be thinking what I know you're thinking."

"Are you serious?" William finally asked.

"Yes. Why not?" Luke asked. "She's not a little girl anymore, in case you haven't noticed."

"Hey, that's my little cousin you're talking about," William replied and threw Luke a playful punch. Luke blocked it and came up with a right upper cut, which William skillfully blocked. They continued their playful wrestling until they both grew tired. Luke decided he had had enough and wanted to return to the subject of dates for the prom. He held up his hand. "Seriously, William, can you ask Margaret for me?"

"No. You can ask her yourself. Since when did you get shy around girls?" replied William.

"It has nothing to do with being shy. I just wanted to be sure it was okay with you. So…is it okay with you?" Luke asked.

"It's okay by me, but I'm sure my mom will read you the riot act before she gives her okay," replied William.

"That's fine. I'm sure she won't object. I can handle Aunt Edith," Luke replied with a smile. He clearly thought he had control over the female species, and none were immune to his irresistible charm.

Good luck then," William said with resignation. His lips said okay, but his heart felt something totally different. All he could think was, *Luke might be my best friend, but I certainly don't trust him with Margaret. His track record with girls is a bit too sordid for my taste. I love Luke like a brother, but I want someone better for Margaret. He has no plans for the future, and the last thing I wish is to see her rush headlong into an uncertain future with Luke.*

Deep down he wished that his mom would refuse to let Margaret go to the prom with Luke.

5

Margaret was relaxing on the sofa in the family room watching television when Luke and William came clattering down the stairs. Margaret stared at them angrily.

"Can't you two be quiet for a minute? I'm trying to watch TV." Ignoring her request, Luke threw himself down on the opposite sofa, his long legs dangling over the arm. "Hey, Margaret, I have a question for you."

Margaret turned and gave him a questioning look. "About what?" she asked angrily. Luke hesitated. Margaret was losing her patience, so again she asked, "So what do you want to ask me?"

"Would you like to go to the prom with me?" Luke finally asked.

Margaret's heartbeat escalated, but she quickly tamped down her anxiety. "Why are you asking me? Did you get the big chill from the girls in your home room?" she asked.

Luke guffawed in reply. "No, I didn't ask anyone. I wanted to ask you first."

"And if I say no?" asked Margaret.

"Then I would take my broken heart and reluctantly ask someone else. But you are the first, believe me," replied Luke, his right hand over his heart, looking as penitent as he could.

He stared at her and winked, giving her one of his drop-dead smiles. Margaret could feel herself drowning in the depths of his big blue eyes. She could not help herself. She hurriedly closed her eyes, tearing her attention away from the magnet that kept threatening to pull her in. She already knew what her answer would be, but she wanted to let him sweat for a while. She pretended to be thinking over her answer; after all, she did not want him thinking she was too easy. Finally, she decided to take him out of his misery and give him an answer.

"Okay, I'll say yes for now, but I'll have to talk to my aunt before I give you my final answer."

Luke smiled at her. "Don't keep me waiting."

Sitting in the chair next to the window, William groaned inwardly at Margaret's response. He was hoping against hope that she would refuse him, but his luck did not seem to be holding.

I hope this is a nightmare that I'll soon wake up from, he thought to himself.

Margaret appeared calm as she continued watching TV, but inside, the butterflies were already having a field day. She couldn't wait to tell her best friend, Sarah. She knew that Sarah had her eyes on William, and she really hoped he would ask her to the prom.

The following day, William got up the courage to ask Sarah. "Yes, I'd love to go to the prom with you," she replied happily. She couldn't wait to tell Margaret.

6

After getting William's solemn promise that he would keep his eyes on Margaret, Aunt Edith reluctantly agreed for Margaret to go to the prom with Luke. Little did she know that she would eventually regret that decision, but she hated to deny Margaret anything that would bring her joy. That one single decision would prove to be the beginning of the end for Margaret, but at the moment, who knew? The two couples had a wonderful time at the prom, and Margaret wished that the night would never end. Both William and Sarah had their futures already mapped out, and so they agreed they would maintain a platonic friendship.

Saying that William loved computers would be an understatement. His whole world revolved around every aspect of computer technology. He was enthusiastic about each and every new version and application to his Microsoft gadgets. It was understood that he would be going to college in the fall and majoring in computer science. However, it came as a big surprise when he announced at the dinner table one night, "Mom and Dad, I just received a letter today. I have to leave for college earlier than planned. There's a specialized course in computers being given this summer, and I can't afford to miss it."

"Does this means you'll be gone for the entire summer?" his mother asked dejectedly.

"I'm afraid so, Mom," replied William.

"But why can't you take that course next semester?" his mother asked sadly.

"This is a course that's not given too often, Mom, and I don't want to miss out. But I promise I'll call home often, and if I can make it home before the fall semester starts, I'll certainly try."

And so the mad rush began getting William ready to leave for college. Visits to the mall had now become a daily event. Shopping bags from every store were now present in the house along with boxes of every shape and size. When the day arrived for William's departure, there was not a dry eye in the Stewart household. Everyone helped with packing William's car, making sure he had all his favorite techy toys, which he thought he couldn't live without. Both Luke and William's dad were accompanying William to help with the unpacking, but most of all they needed a car for the drive back home.

As the last piece of luggage was loaded into William's car, his mother came out to hug him good-bye.

"William," she said, tears in her eyes. "Don't forget to call home. I'm really going to miss you," she continued as tears streamed down her face unashamedly.

William returned her hug. "I'm going to miss you too, Mom, but I'll call home often, I promise," he choked out. She held on tight to William, refusing to let go. His dad gently but forcibly removed her arms from around William's neck and lovingly kissed her tear-stained face.

"He'll be home soon, Edith, and we can always go to visit him," he said soothingly. It broke his heart to see her sad, so he enveloped her in his big, strong arms, hoping to soothe her and help lessen her pain.

Finally, it was Margaret's turn to say good-bye. She dried her eyes before hugging William, but the tears returned as soon as he returned her hug. He took her by the hand, leading her away so he could talk to her without being overheard. "Margaret," said

William, the words sticking in his throat. Clearing his throat, he tried again. "Margaret, I have one favor to ask."

Margaret looked him in the eyes. "What is it, William? You know I'll do anything for you," she said.

William finally found his voice. "I know that right now you're not thinking about college, but please promise me you'll give it some serious thought. I know you care about Luke, but there is no future with him, and I don't want to see you hurt. You're my little sister, and all I want is what's best for you."

Margaret winced under William's stare, but she had no response to give because deep down she knew he was right. Luke had no future, but how could she help herself? She felt so powerless when she was around him. In a small voice, she finally whispered, "I'll try, William."

William was gone, and Margaret and Luke were now inseparable. Much to her aunt's chagrin, they now spent every spare moment together. William's request would often come to Margaret's mind, but much as she tried, she just couldn't stay away from Luke. He was like a magnet that kept beckoning her to him, and she lacked the willpower to deny him. She was never happier than when they were driving around town in Luke's beat-up yellow Mustang or lazing around in his room at his parents' house. This was her last year in high school, and she still remained ambivalent regarding her own future.

Throughout high school, Margaret had shown a strong affinity for numbers, so after class one day, Ms. Collins, her math teacher, pulled her aside. "Margaret, your math skills are excellent. You've always maintained an A average. Please tell me you're majoring in math when you go away to college. There is always a need for good math teachers."

"I don't think I'm going to college," replied Margaret nonchalantly.

Ms. Collins looked perplexed, unsure of what she was hearing. "And why not?" she asked.

"I just don't feel that college is for me," replied Margaret.

"You're making a very big mistake, Margaret. Does your parents know about this?" Not waiting for a response, Ms. Collins continued. "You're willing to waste all that talent you've been given? So what are your plans if you're not going to college?" she continued in amazement.

Margaret shrugged her shoulders. "I don't know. Maybe I'll get a job. I can always go to college later."

Ms. Collins shook her head sadly. "You're making such a big mistake. You need to think seriously about your future, Margaret."

Her teachers were not the only ones disappointed in Margaret's decision. Her aunt and uncle were extremely disappointed and had, on more than one occasion, discussed the subject with her.

"A high school diploma won't take you very far these days, Margaret," her aunt had told her.

However, she remained adamant about postponing college, and nothing they said would sway her from that decision.

After a lot of encouragement from Margaret, Luke enrolled at the local community college. Not knowing exactly what he wanted to do with his life, he decided to major in liberal arts. He was unsure what he would do with a degree in liberal arts, but he went along for the ride. His heart was not in it, and he struggled with almost every subject. Several times he thought about dropping out, but Margaret encouraged him to continue, at least on a part-time basis, and so he did. During his spare time, he hung out at the local garage and never looked in his textbooks until it was time for the next class.

Little by little, Margaret started seeing subtle changes in Luke. He was often moody, blaming it on William's absence. "I miss William. I had no idea I'd miss him this much," was his reply whenever Margaret asked him what was troubling him. Margaret did all she could to take his mind off his problem, but her efforts only worked for a short time. Eventually, the dark mood would return.

"You seem happiest when you're meddling with cars. Why don't you enroll in auto mechanic school? You could probably earn a good livelihood from fixing cars," Margaret asked him once.

"I don't want to work for other people all my life," he replied.

"Who says that you have to? You could own your garage one of these days, but you have to start somewhere."

"Well, it's probably worth thinking about," he replied. After much thought, Luke took Margaret's advice. He dropped out of college and enrolled at a technical school where he started courses in auto mechanic while working part time at the garage. He still lived at his parents' house, but did his best to save toward one day getting his own place.

7

Margaret was now eighteen, and graduation time was here. She still had no plans for college, and William's advice had long since gone out the window. Graduation day came and went, and the summer was flying by on wings. Fall was fast approaching, and it would soon be time for her friend Sarah to leave for college. Sarah had been accepted to Brighton College and planned to major in her favorite subject, English. She and Margaret had decided to meet for lunch at their favorite diner the day before she left for Brighton.

"Let's not talk about college until after we eat," Margaret said to Sarah as they slid into their favorite booth. "I want to postpone saying good-bye for as long as possible." They had a leisurely lunch, reminiscing in between mouthfuls about high school and all the years they had known each other.

"Let's take a walk in the park like we used to," Sarah suggested after lunch.

"Why not? Let's go," replied Margaret. They headed into the park and strolled along familiar paths that brought back so many happy memories, but hidden beneath this facade of happiness, Sarah was deeply concerned about Margaret. She was so overcome with emotion she stopped in her track. She turned and looked at Margaret, her love for her friend all over her face.

"What happened to you, Meg?" she asked with concern. "Remember when we used to talk about going away to college together?" continued Sarah. Margaret looked everywhere except on Sarah's face. She just couldn't face her friend.

"I'm going to miss you, Meg," Sarah continued sadly. "I don't know why you're not coming with me. We should be leaving together." Margaret shrugged.

"Well, things change, Sarah. I no longer have the desire to go to college. You're the smart one," she said, pushing at Sarah playfully.

"You're smart too," replied Sarah, pushing back. "I remember when I had to come to you for help with math." Sarah's tone became serious as she looked into her friend's eyes. "Please don't waste your life, Meg. Things may seem great with Luke right now, but…" she broke off and wiped tears from her eyes before trying again. "I hope you don't take this the wrong way, Meg, but Luke has no future plans. You're too smart to be just frittering your life away with him." She paused to clear the hitch in her throat. "Anyway, I hope you give this a lot of thought."

"Yeah, I'll think about it," Margaret replied. They hugged for a long time, so many memories running through their heads. They finally pulled apart, both wiping their eyes. Sarah looked at Margaret, and in a voice ready to break, she said, "I don't know what else to say, Meg. I'm leaving in the morning, and I don't think I'll see you before I go." She took a deep breath before continuing. "I'll call you when I can, but remember what I said. It's never too late, Meg."

"I'll keep it in mind," Margaret replied.

They hugged again and headed in opposite directions.

8

Margaret remained mesmerized by Luke Foster. It was clear that he was going nowhere, and he was taking Margaret along with him for the ride. She was just too blinded by her obsession to see clearly.

It deeply pained Margaret's aunt and uncle to see her wasting her life and talents by refusing to go to college. Together they discussed it and decided that it was past time to confront Margaret.

"I'll talk to her," her aunt decided.

"No," Albert interjected. "After all, she's my brother's daughter."

"I know she is, but I think that's my job," replied Edith.

After much discussion, they decided they would do it together. It was after midnight when Margaret came home. Her aunt and uncle were waiting up for her. "Margaret, your uncle and I need to speak with you," her aunt said as Margaret entered the house.

Margaret started in surprise. "Aunt Edith, Uncle Albert, what are you doing in the dark? It's late. You should be asleep by now."

"Your uncle and I have been trying to find the best time to talk to you, but you're usually out all day, so we decided we'd wait up," replied her aunt.

Her aunt reached for the light switch and turned on the lamp on the side table. As the light penetrated the darkness, Margaret tried hiding her face in the shadows cast by the lamp. However, she was not quick enough to escape her aunt's eagle eyes. Aunt

Edith took a quick breath as she caught sight of the bruise on Margaret's left cheek.

"You're hurt," she said, getting up from her chair and attempting to go to Margaret. "What happened to your face? Did Luke do that to you?"

"No," Margaret replied angrily, starting to leave the room. "Luke would never hurt me. It's just a scratch," she said, still hiding her face.

"How did it happen?" asked her uncle.

"Luke and I were goofing around, and I fell and hit my face. It's not a big deal," she said defensively. "Anyway, what did you want to talk about?"

Her aunt took a long, hard look at her but decided not to pursue the subject. "Why don't you sit?" her aunt invited.

"I think I'll stand," replied Margaret, standing with her arms folded.

"Okay, that's your choice," replied her aunt.

"Well, now that you've graduated from high school and you have no plans to go to college, your uncle and I believe it's time you found a job," her aunt began. Margaret took a breath but said nothing, so her aunt continued.

"If you're going to continue living here, then you need to contribute to the household expenses. While you were in high school, we were quite willing to pay. If you were in college, we would also be willing to pay. However, since you've decided to waste your life, we can no longer afford to support you—"

Margaret cut in sharply, aghast at what she was hearing. "Contribute to the household? Do you mean you want me to pay rent?"

"Well, yes, if that's what you choose to call it. It's time you became more responsible. You can't expect that someone will be caring for you the rest of your life. Furthermore, your uncle and I aren't getting any younger, and the cold and snow is starting to get to us. So we've been thinking about moving to some place warmer. We would love to see you settled in a place of your own, get a nice job, or start college before we relocate."

Margaret could not believe what she was hearing. Her anger mounted at the thought of having to pay rent in the home she had lived in for the past thirteen years. She clenched her hands into tight fists to prevent them from shaking.

"I'll be out of here by the end of the week." She tossed over her shoulder before angrily storming off and quickly running up the stairs. The slamming of her bedroom door reverberated throughout the entire house.

9

For the next few days, Margaret was scarcely seen by her aunt or uncle. The only time they knew of her presence in the house was when they heard her sneaking in after midnight. She was usually up and out of the house before they came down to breakfast the next morning.

"I wonder where she goes all day," her uncle said thoughtfully.

"Where else but with Luke? That girl is such a disappointment. I had such high hopes for her. I wish I had said no when she asked to go to the prom with that Luke Foster. That's when it all seemed to have started," Aunt Edith continued. She sighed as a deep sadness suffused her face. Uncle Albert took one look at her, pulled her closer to him, and gave her a tight hug. *I agree wholeheartedly, youth is indeed wasted on the young,* he thought.

One week later, Aunt Edith and Uncle Albert were relaxing in the den watching their favorite show, "As Time Goes By." They were both ardent lovers of British television, especially the comedies. They tried their best not to miss a single episode. However, whenever they were unable to watch the weekly episodes, they would record and watch them at their leisure. This episode was especially one of their favorites, and they had watched it a number of times but never seemed to tire of it. They were watching the episode where Lionel and Jean had just been reconciled after years of being apart. Lionel had taken Jean on a picnic with Judy and Alistair. Lionel was kissing Jean when he suddenly realized he needed to use the restroom. Aunt Edith and Uncle Albert were both laughing at Lionel's dry humor when the doorbell interrupted.

"I wonder who that could be," Uncle Albert asked angrily.

"See who it is, Albert, and get rid of them fast," Aunt Edith replied. Albert reluctantly got up from his chair and looked through the peephole. "It's Margaret and Luke. I wonder what they want," he whispered.

"Well, open the door. The faster we find out what they want, the faster we can get back to watching our show," replied Aunt Edith. Uncle Albert opened the door reluctantly, and Luke and Margaret entered, smiling and holding hands. "Hi, Auntie. Hi, Uncle. Luke and I have some great news," Margaret gushed. She could hardly contain herself.

"Have a seat and tell us your news," said Aunt Edith. Still holding hands, they quickly sat down on the love seat. It was evident that Margaret's news was burning a hole in her heart. No sooner had they sat down than Margaret quickly stuck out her left hand. A shiny new wedding band sparkled on her ring finger. Unable to contain her joy any longer, she quickly blurted out, "Luke and I just got married." Her aunt and uncle looked from one to the other and then back at Margaret and Luke, unsure if they should offer their well-wishes or ask if they had lost their minds.

"When did this happen?" her aunt asked after regaining her voice.

"Today," Margaret piped up. "We're just on our way back from the city clerk's office. Do you like my ring?" she asked excitedly, splaying her fingers for them to see.

"It's very beautiful," her aunt replied hesitantly.

"This is a surprise. When did you plan this?" asked her uncle.

"It was a spur-of-the-moment decision, but we both knew it would happen eventually. Better sooner than later," Margaret replied, looking lovingly at Luke.

"Well, good luck to you both," said her aunt hesitantly. She kept looking from one to the other questioningly until finally she could contain herself no longer. "I have to ask this question. Now that you're man and wife, where will you both be living?" An uncomfortable silence descended as the newlyweds shuffled in their seats.

"Well, I'm sure you've thought about this before you jumped into it. Marriage is a big responsibility. How are you going to support yourselves? Have you thought about that?" She continued looking at them, but no one volunteered a response.

"Would anyone like a drink?" Uncle Albert asked, trying to break the uncomfortable silence.

"Yes, please," both Margaret and Luke replied as one. Uncle Albert hurried off to the kitchen, happy to escape the tension-laden living room. He soon returned with a tray of drinks and handed them all around. However, the conversation was still absent, and the room remained thick with unspoken words. Sadly, no one drank to the young couple's health or happiness. The newlyweds left shortly after, heading for Luke's parents' house.

10

A year passed by, and Margaret was now nineteen, married, and living in a rented apartment not far from the house she had known as home. She rarely, if ever, saw her aunt or uncle. Sadly she had made her decision not to visit them, and respecting her decision, her aunt and uncle had also chosen not to visit them.

Luke was a loving and devoted husband, and they spent lots of time talking about the large family they both wanted. "I want lots of babies," Luke told Margaret.

"I can't wait," Margaret said happily as she snuggled up close. "I don't want our kids to be lonely. Oh, we're going to be so happy!"

"I don't want you working," Luke told her. "I don't want the mother of my children working for anyone but me. I want you to stay home and look pretty for me when I get home," he told her jokingly.

Time passed, and Margaret settled into her new role of being a stay-at-home wife. She loved being Luke's wife, and being a housewife was everything she wanted. The only ruffle on the sea of their tranquil marriage was Margaret's inability to conceive. Each month brought new hope, only to have them dashed when the abdominal cramps started, summoning her monthly period. Each visit to the doctor just brought more heartache. However, their gynecologist, Dr. Cohen, never gave up hope and was always very supportive.

"Just relax, Margaret. Let nature take its course," he advised kindly. "Your physical exams and tests so far are normal, and I see no reason why you should not have babies the normal way." With each visit, the news was the same, and they would both return home disappointed and discouraged.

"I think we should have Luke tested, just to be sure," Dr. Cohen suggested at their next visit. This annoyed Luke to no end. "I'm fine. I don't need to be tested. Nothing's wrong with me," he responded angrily.

"I'm not saying anything's wrong with you, Luke," said Dr. Cohen patiently, "but we should cover all the bases. This is just the final piece of the puzzle to find out why Margaret is not getting pregnant." But despite all the explanations and the coaxing, Luke remained adamant and refused to be tested.

It was now approaching there second wedding anniversary, and it was now obvious that being parents the normal way was not going to happen. That's when Margaret started to see a different side of Luke Foster; a side that she both feared and loathed. Not long after, he started drinking and staying out late.

"Why are you staying out so late? I'm lonely here by myself," Margaret said to him as he dragged himself in from the garage late one evening. "Give me some babies, and I'll have a reason to come home," he replied angrily.

Margaret cringed each time she felt the slightest twinge of abdominal discomfort. It didn't matter if it was related to a digestive disorder or a bout of anxiety, she dreaded it all just the same. She was constantly in a state of nervousness, and this did nothing to raise Luke's spirits or to increase her chances of getting pregnant. In fact, at times Margaret scarcely recognized the man she had married.

On the day of their anniversary, Margaret decided they would celebrate in style, such as they could afford. As she busied herself with the preparations, she hoped Luke would be in a good mood. After all, this was supposed to be a special occasion.

Maybe we'll even work on getting pregnant, she smiled to herself at the thought. It was Saturday, and Luke had gone in to work, but Margaret was looking forward to a romantic night for a change. She had been working hard all day getting things ready for a wonderful evening. "I hope he remembers that it's our anniversary," she said to herself as she put on her nicest dress.

"This is an important day for both of us. I hope he surprises me with a nice gift." As she looked in the mirror at her bare neck, she kept hoping. *Custom jewelry is so much in style these days. They're so beautiful; I really love them. A silver necklace would go nicely with my outfits, and they cost so much less than gold.*

She had cooked Luke's favorite meal of spaghetti and meatballs, set the table with the best dishes they possessed, and had even bought some fresh-cut flowers. Last but not least, she had even sprung for a bottle of inexpensive wine.

Luke was late getting home from work, which was not unusual, but Margaret had kept hoping with all her heart that today would be different. As soon as she heard his key in the lock, she quickly ran to the door. She was disappointed when she saw his hands were empty, but she was hopeful nonetheless.

Maybe he bought my gift earlier and hid it someplace to surprise me, she thought.

She could smell the alcohol on his breath the moment he entered the apartment. Margaret's heart fell to the floor, but she hid it well. "Happy anniversary." She smiled, trying her best to put on a brave face while hiding the fear.

"What anniversary?" Luke slurred, looking at her sideways. Not waiting for a reply, he stumbled his way into the kitchen. He spotted the bottle of wine on the table. He picked it up and weaved toward Margaret. Barely able to get the words out, he asked, "How much…did you pay for this…?"

"It was not expensive," Margaret replied fearfully.

"Where did you get the money?" he shouted. "We can't afford to waste money on fancy wine. You…better take it back."

Margaret cowered in a corner as he weaved about the room. She wondered how he had been able to drive home without getting in an accident. "Luke," she begged. "Please sit before you fall and hurt yourself."

He finally settled in a chair at the dinner table. By this time, Margaret was very close to tears. She served the meal with trembling hands and a heavy heart, trying hard to hold back the tears. After serving him, she finally sat down, but her appetite was long gone. She picked at her food, which just served to enrage Luke. "Who's going to eat all this food?" he asked, looking at the table. "This is just more money down the drain," he continued. The more he raged, the more fearful Margaret became. She had had enough of Luke's tyranny for one night, so she decided she might as well go to bed.

Almost in tears, she got up from the table. "I'm going to bed," she said. She was in the process of replacing the chair under the table when Luke suddenly lunged toward her. The sudden movement caught her off guard as Luke roughly grabbed hold of her arm. She tried to pull away, but the harder she pulled, the tighter he held on. Alcohol seemed to have given him superhuman strength.

So intent was she on releasing herself from his grasp, she failed to see him raise his right hand. As his fist landed on her face, she staggered backward and fell. As she fell, the back of her head connected with the sharp edge of the dining table. She fell to the floor, still and unmoving. Blood gushed from the gash to her head as well as from her nose where Luke's punch had landed. The presence of blood seemed to cause Luke to quickly regain his sobriety. He fell to his knees beside her and shook her by the shoulder. "Meg, Meg, wake up. Please don't die. I'm so sorry, baby. Please wake up. I'm sorry, I didn't mean it. I'll never do it again."

Margaret did not respond. Luke cradled her in his arms, shaking her and calling her name. "Margaret, honey, please wake up. It was the alcohol. If you wake up, I promise I'll never drink again." For what seemed an eternity, Luke kept shaking her, but she remained unresponsive. The carpet was soaked with blood, which just served to frighten Luke more. Unsure of what to do and thinking she might die, he pulled out his cell phone and dialed 911.

"911, what's your emergency?" the telephone operator asked.

In his nervousness, he could barely get the words out. "It's my wife...she...she fell and hit her head. She's bleeding from her nose too. There's blood everywhere...Could you send an ambulance, please?"

"Is she conscious, sir?"

"Yes. No. I don't know," replied Luke, crying nervously.

"Make sure she's lying down. Turn her on her side so she won't aspirate."

"As...aspirate? What does that mean?" asked Luke nervously.

"Turn her on her side so she won't choke on her blood, sir."

"Okay, okay. Is the ambulance on the way?" asked Luke in panic.

"Sir, what is your address?" asked the operator.

"Ah...243 Pike Place, apartment 24, we're on the second floor. Please hurry."

Before Luke finished talking to the operator, he could hear the sound of the ambulance in the distance.

11

Luke hurriedly opened the door and led the paramedics to where Margaret was lying on the kitchen floor as pale as a ghost. Full consciousness had still not returned; she was still unresponsive to touch or any other type of stimulation. Her color seemed to have gotten much paler as a result of the blood loss. As one paramedic quickly checked her vital signs and start an intravenous fluid, the other turned his attention to the wound.

"What happened, sir? How did she sustain her injury?" one of the paramedics asked as they prepared to load her onto the gurney. Luke's clothing was covered with Margaret's blood, but he was unaware as he hovered over her, ever the loving and concerned husband. "She was going upstairs and stubbed her toe on the table and fell," he said quickly.

"Did she hit her head or her nose?" the paramedic asked skeptically.

"I don't know," Luke replied defensively. "It all happened so fast. Will she be okay?"

"Sir, we're doing all we can for her. We'll stabilize her, but we need to get her to the Emergency Room as soon as possible. The doctor can give you more information as soon as he examines her. Would you like to come with us in the ambulance, or follow in your car?" asked the paramedic. Luke thought for a minute, then decided he would follow them in his car. "Okay, you can follow us in your car. Just don't run any red lights," the paramedic warned.

Keeping the paramedics warning in mind, Luke followed behind the ambulance. When he finally pulled into the closest parking space to the emergency entrance, the paramedics had already rolled the gurney into one of the cubicles, and Margaret was being examined by Dr. Meyer, the ER physician. A very concerned Luke hurried into the cubicle, "Will she be okay, Doctor?" he asked.

"Well, as soon as I finish examining her, I can give you all the details, sir. Are you her husband?" Dr. Meyer asked, looking at Luke's bloody clothes.

"Yes, I am," Luke replied nervously.

The doctor and nurse were bent over the gurney. Margaret was slowly regaining consciousness and was moaning at intervals. The IV fluid was now running at a fairly rapid rate into her right arm, and her color was no longer that sickly grey.

"Do you remember what happened to you, Ms. Foster?" the nurse asked. Luke was standing by the gurney holding Margaret's hands. Margaret attempted to speak, but Luke was faster with his answer.

"She was going to bed because she was tired. That's when she stubbed her toe and fell against the edge of the table. We were celebrating our second wedding anniversary, and I think she might have had a little too much to drink. She's not used to drinking," he smiled conspiratorially at the doctor. "I don't think she remembers everything. She's still in shock," he continued, looking with concern at the nurse and doctor standing by the bed. The doctor and nurse exchanged covert looks. "We'd like Ms. Foster to answer the question, if you don't mind, Mr. Foster," the nurse said.

"I'm just trying to help my wife. I love her so much," Luke replied, trying to hug a moaning Margaret.

"We understand that sir, but I need to hear her responses to my questions in order to gauge her level of consciousness," said Dr. Meyer. "I know you're very concerned about her, sir, but I need to examine her physically as well as neurologically. It's the only way I can determine my mode of treatment. Now, sir, can you please wait outside until I've finished my exam?" asked the doctor.

Luke reluctantly stepped out of the cubicle but made sure he was not too far away. He wanted to be able to hear every question asked and every response given. He stood by the cubicle, his ears attuned to every sound and movement behind the curtains.

The doctor finally emerged from behind the curtain, accompanied by the nurse. They didn't have to look too far to find Luke. He was lingering near the cubicle. "Mr. Foster, I'll need to keep your wife overnight for observation. We also need to run more tests and take some x-rays just to make sure we're not missing anything."

"I-I can take care of her at home," Luke said nervously. "I'll make sure she's okay," he said, looking steadfastly at the doctor.

The doctor shook his head. "Sorry, Mr. Foster, this is hospital policy. Your wife sustained a head injury. She was unconscious for a long while, in addition to losing quite a lot of blood. She needs constant observation in case she lapses into a coma. If I sent her home and she became unconscious and dies at home, you would be the first to bring a lawsuit against both me and the hospital for sending her home too soon. Sorry, Mr. Foster, she stays," said the doctor determinedly. He gave Luke a look which said "I mean exactly what I say."

"But I'll watch her carefully…" Luke started. The doctor had said his piece, so he started walking away. "Sorry, Mr. Foster, but this conversation is over."

"I guess I'll have no choice but to stay with her," said Luke to himself. "I don't want them asking her too many questions when I'm not around."

12

Margaret gradually woke up, opened her eyes, and tried focusing on her surroundings. "Where am I?" she asked groggily.

Luke quickly got up from his chair and bent close to her. "Margaret," he whispered. "I'm here. Are you okay?"

Margaret held on to her head and moaned. "Oh, my head. It hurts so…" Before she finished the sentence, vomitus spurted from her mouth, showering Luke from his shirt all the way down to his shoes. For a moment, his anger flared, but he quickly caught himself. Giving her a look that was less than sympathetic, he ran from behind the curtain and called out, "Nurse, nurse! Please, my wife is vomiting."

The nurse hurried over, closed the curtain, and asked Luke to wait outside. Margaret was sitting up in bed, her color pale and her skin diaphoretic.

"Margaret, how are you feeling?" the nurse asked sympathetically.

"Nauseous," she replied as she continued retching.

"Don't worry, you'll be okay. Is there anything else I should know?" the nurse asked, trying to keep her head elevated.

"The whole room is spinning, and my head feels as if I'm in a fog," replied Margaret.

"That's not unusual after you've sustained a head injury," the nurse continued. "But don't worry, you'll be okay. It's all part of the process." She removed the soiled sheets and gown, allowed Margaret to rinse her mouth, and made her comfortable before leaving. As soon as her vital signs stabilized, she was transferred to the medical observation unit on the third floor where she would remain until she was ready for discharge home.

Margaret's tests showed she had sustained a mild concussion, so staying for observation and monitoring was routine procedure for the hospital. By Tuesday, all her nausea was gone along with the headaches and dizziness. Neurologically she was ready for discharge, but it was her physical safety that remained a major concern to both Margaret and the nursing staff.

Late Tuesday evening, Dr. Mason, one of the Residents on the observation unit and Jill, her nurse sat with Luke and Margaret to give them discharge instructions. Dr. Mason strongly cautioned them both regarding her care at home. "She needs time to rest in order to completely heal," he told them both. "As a rule, people with mild concussion usually recover fully. Luckily, her concussion was not very severe, so I believe she will be fine if you follow my instructions."

Looking directly at Luke, Jill interjected, "It won't be unusual if she complains of headaches, difficulty with concentration and memory, balance, and coordination. These will only be temporary, but if they persist, then you need to bring her back to the ER immediately, especially if she becomes nauseous and starts vomiting."

"How soon will she be able to do things around the house?" Luke asked.

Dr. Mason tried his best to maintain his patience. For some unknown reason, he was still convinced that Luke had contributed in some way to Margaret's accident. However, he had no way of proving his suspicions, but that did not mean he had to like or trust Luke.

"Did you hear what I just said?" he asked. "It usually takes about a week for things to return to normal. I'm aware that every person is different, and the time it takes to recover from a concussion is also different for each individual. So let her heal as nature allows."

"Do you have any questions for me, Margaret?" Jill asked, looking at her sympathetically.

"No, I can't think of any," replied Margaret.

"Do you have anyone who can assist you around the house while you're recuperating? Any family members living close by?" asked Jill.

Margaret nodded. "Yes, my aunt lives close by. She'll help me if I ask."

Not if I have anything to say about that, thought Luke to himself.

"Okay, if there are no further questions, someone will take you in a wheelchair to your car." said Jill.

"That's okay, D, I can manage," Luke piped up.

Dr. Mason looked at him patiently. "It's hospital policy, Mr. Foster. Let us do our job, please."

Luke drove Margaret home and had her comfortably settled in no time. He hovered over her, ever the devoted husband, responding to Margaret's every beck and call. Margaret, however, had very little to say as so many thoughts kept swirling around in her head.

The following morning, Luke reluctantly prepared for work as he was unable to get the day off. Before leaving home, he made sure Margaret had everything she needed.

"Don't worry about a thing, Meg. I'll be back early with dinner. Do you have anything special in mind?" he asked.

"Chinese food sounds good," replied Margaret.

"Don't let your aunt and uncle find out about what happened. I'm sure they'll think that I did this to you," he warned her.

"Well, you did," Margaret said softly.

Luke looked at her with fire in his eyes, and with hands clenched, he walked toward her. Margaret cowered on the sofa. He bent and kissed her on her cheek, turned, and left the apartment without another word.

Margaret had youth on her side, so she was back to her normal self within a short time. However, left at home by herself, she had nothing but time on her hands for introspection and soul searching. She started looking at her life from so many different perspectives. "What have I accomplished in my life?" she asked herself. *Nothing* was the reply.

"I live in constant fear, never knowing what mood Luke will be in when he gets home. I shudder whenever I hear his key in the front door. This is all my fault. I should have listened to William and Sarah and gone to college when I had the chance. How could he have changed so much? Why didn't I see this side of him before?"

"Luke never wanted me to work outside the home, thinking I should stay home and raise a family. Of course, I thought that by this time I would be a mother too. Seems like that's not going to happen! So what's next? It's not my fault I can't have children." She kept walking around the apartment, frustrated at herself. "I know there's more to life than this," she continued. Her mind continued racing, but she could see no immediate solution to her present condition. She had no job and no skills. All she had were a few dollars she had managed to put aside from the money Luke gave her for groceries.

Soon another year rolled by, and Margaret continued drifting along with no concrete plans for her future. Although Luke was now working full time at the garage, financially they were barely getting by. He had dropped out of auto mechanic school and refused to entertain the subject whenever Margaret raised it. If fact, it was just another of the many subjects that was taboo in their apartment; and believe me, there were so, so many. Whenever Margaret mentioned the possibility of finding a job, Luke's anger would surface. Despite the limited income, he had recently bought Margaret a small used car. Her feeling of independence knew no bounds as she was now able to get from one place to the next without feeling completely dependent on him.

Margaret was now a frequent visitor at the Plains Hospital emergency room for one incident after the next. However, try as they might, the ER staff could not convince her to tell the truth about how she sustained her injuries. She had become an expert liar.

13

Margaret had never been a religious person. She barely recalled going to church with her parents when they were alive, but it was a vague memory. As for her aunt and uncle, they were not churchgoers, and so she had never felt motivated to attend. However, at the moment, she desperately felt the need for some divine intervention, and she was not shy about asking for it.

"Oh God," she prayed. "I don't know the right way to pray, but I desperately need your help. I know I have not always been good, but please tell me what to do. I'm so sorry I've been wasting my talents, but if you would just give me one more chance, Lord, I promise I'll make up for everything."

Despite her prayers, her feeling of desolation persisted. She had not talked to her friend Sarah in a long time, and she had no other close friends in whom to confide. As for her aunt and uncle, she had chosen to distance herself from them. In fact, she was not even sure they were still living in Plains.

In desperation, she asked herself. *How did my life become such a mess?*

It was Monday morning and autumn was in the air. It was Margaret's least favorite time of year, and already she could sense the feelings of sadness and foreboding settling deep into her soul. Luke hated coming home to an untidy house, so she busied herself with the usual monotonous household chores of dusting and mopping. She desperately wanted Luke not to find a reason to lose his temper when he got home.

"Other women lead busy lives," she said as she dusted the furniture in the dining room. "I wish I had a job to go to even on a part-time basis. I'm sure it would be something to look forward to. It's not as if we couldn't use the money, but Luke and his damn pride," she said angrily. "Every time I mention getting a job, he goes berserk." She threw down her dusting cloth in anger and sat down on the living room sofa. "I can't do this anymore. This is not living, it's existing. I refuse to do this anymore."

She sent up a silent prayer asking for a solution. Suddenly, it was as if a light bulb went off over her head. She knew what she must do! The solution was right in front of her, and so there and then, she made her decision. With this new clarity of mind, she was suddenly surrounded by a wonderful sense of calm.

She was in excellent spirits when Luke arrived home. He took one look at her, and with his head tilted to one side, he asked. "What's going on? You're in a good mood this evening."

"Oh, nothing," she replied and continued humming as she prepared dinner. Having had a few drinks on his way home, he was spoiling for a fight, and Margaret could sense it. Thinking that she was hiding something from him, something that he would not approve of, he decided to find out the only way he knew how.

"I'll give you something to sing about," he growled as he lunged across the table toward her. From the corner of her eyes, Margaret saw him move toward her. She tried moving away, but she was not fast enough. Before she realized what was happening, she felt his hands around her throat squeezing hard. Almost at the point of blacking out, she gathered one last ounce of strength and elbowed him hard in the ribs.

He released his grip and doubled over trying to catch his breath. This gave Margaret the chance she needed. She took a deep breath, coughed, then ducked and ran, grabbing her purse and car keys as she headed out the door. Her car could be temperamental at times, sometimes refusing to start. She hoped that today would not be one of those days. She prayed as she fumbled to get the key into the ignition. She turned the key, and to her relief, the engine turned over at the first try. She shifted into drive and literally flew down the driveway, missing Luke by an inch as he tried to block her way. She headed down the street as if her life depended on it.

Reaching the intersection, she quickly glanced in the rearview mirror, and to her horror, she saw Luke's yellow mustang barreling down upon her. She knew she was going over the speed limit, but that was the least of her problems. Life was more important. She was fast approaching the drawbridge but had no intention of slowing down.

"Dear God, please hear me. I need you now more than ever," she prayed as she took the steep curve leading onto the bridge.

As the drawbridge loomed in sight, she could see the center of the bridge starting to separate. A quick glance in the rearview mirror told her that Luke was gaining on her. A sudden surge of adrenaline gave her the strength she needed, so she gunned the engine for all it was worth. Closer and closer to the bridge she came, and with one last desperate push on the gas pedal, she was airborne! She closed her eyes and held on to the steering wheel as she flew through the air. With what seemed like a lifetime, she remained suspended. Suddenly she landed with a clatter on the opposite side of the bridge. She applied the brakes and quickly looked back, amazed at what had just happened. She quickly opened her car door and ran toward the railing. She was just in time to see Luke's yellow mustang go airborne for a second then plunge into the rapidly moving water below. The yellow mustang was swiftly floating downstream with the tide. She watched for a while not believing what she was seeing. She covered her eyes, not wanting to see the final end to her nightmare.

Soon a crowd started gathering, and thinking that someone would make the 911 call, she quietly returned to her car. Sitting quietly in her car, a myriad of emotions flooded her body. She was unsure if her tears were those of joy or of sorrow. One thing she knew for sure was by the time she had shed her last tear, darkness had almost descended. She shivered as the chilly autumn cold penetrated through to her bones as it were. In her haste to flee, she had forgotten to grab her coat, but when you're fleeing for your life, a coat was not a priority. Rousing herself, she continued to the exit for the highway north, not knowing what lay ahead, only aware that she had no other choice but to keep moving.

14

With the car heater at maximum, Margaret drove for what seemed like hours, not knowing where she was or where she would eventually end up. Fear had taken away her appetite, but darkness seemed to have brought it back.

Checking her watch, she was surprised to see it was almost midnight. She took the nearest exit off the highway and pulled into the parking lot of a diner. Trying her best to appear inconspicuous, she entered and found a seat in a quiet corner. She was happy that the diner was almost empty as she did not feel much like talking. She picked up a menu and tried to decide what she should eat.

"I really don't feel hungry, but I guess I should eat something. On second thought, a bowl of soup would really take the chill off," she said to herself. A waitress soon approached, so she looked up from the menu and asked. "What's the name of this town?"

"Sycamore," the waitress replied. Seeing the blank look on Margaret's face, the waitress continued, "Sycamore, Connecticut! You must be new around here."

"Yes, I am," replied Margaret, using her scarf to try and cover the bruises on her neck. "Is there an inexpensive hotel around here where I can stay the night?"

"In Sycamore?" the waitress replied with a laugh. "You *are* new around here. There's nothing inexpensive in Sycamore, but there are hotels off the highway in the next town, about four or five miles ahead."

Seeing a look that resembled fear cross Margaret's face, the waitress asked kindly. "By the way, it's cold out there. Where's your coat?"

Margaret had almost blocked out the fact that she was cold, but the very mention of the word brought her mind back to her current condition. She hugged herself hoping to generate some body heat, but she couldn't stop herself from trembling or her teeth from chattering.

"Are you in trouble? Can I help?" asked the waitress in a kind voice. Margaret tried to speak, but the tears would not allow her. She tried again but failed miserably. She finally gave up and allowed the tears to fall freely down her face.

"Please don't cry. My name is Carol," the waitress said softly. She took a seat beside Margaret and placed an arm around her shoulder. "Is there anything I can do to help?" she asked quietly. Margaret opened her mouth but no words came out.

"I get off work in half an hour. Stick around, and we can talk then," said Carol, leaving Margaret to attend to other customers. She soon returned with a piping hot bowl of soup. Placing it in front of Margaret, she smiled. "Here, this will help to warm you up."

Margaret nodded as Carol headed off to take the orders of some late-arriving customers. Margaret ate until sated. It was the best-tasting meal she had had all day.

The diner closed at midnight, and after cleaning up in preparation for the next day, Margaret accepted Carol's offer to visit her apartment where they could talk.

I know this is not the smartest thing to do, I don't even know this person, Margaret thought to herself. *But what could be worse than what I just left behind?*

Carol lived only a short distance from the diner. Soon they arrived into an apartment that was very warm, comfortable, and felt so much like home. Margaret rubbed her hands together, trying to get some warmth back into her fingers. Carol quickly found a blanket and wrapped it around her shoulders. "Let me get you some hot tea," said Carol, hurrying off to the kitchen to get the kettle boiling. Sitting at the table in Carol's small kitchen, Margaret felt as if she had lived there all her life. It was so warm and cozy.

"Peppermint tea never tasted so good," she said to Carol as she wrapped her hands against the warm cup.

"I'm glad you're enjoying it," replied Carol.

Soon Margaret was all thawed out, and all she wanted to do was bare her soul. For the first time in a long time, she felt she could speak freely, and she did just that. She told Carol about the unspeakable things she had suffered at the hands of her husband. She cried as she poured her heart out. She had kept silent for so long, never quite trusting herself to tell anyone about the pain she had endured.

For some unknown reason, call it a higher power, their paths had now crossed. Here was Carol, a total stranger who had befriended her when she desperately needed a friend. How could she not reveal to this "stranger-friend" who had rescued her about all the burden she was carrying inside?

As Carol listened to Margaret's story, she couldn't help but shed her own tears. She hugged Margaret hard. "Better days are ahead. That was your test, and you've come through with flying colors. Just keep on praying, and don't you ever give up," she told her. "Why don't you stay the night?" she asked after calm had returned to the room.

Margaret looked skeptical before replying, "I really don't want to impose. I've already bent your ears enough for the night. I can find that hotel if you'll just give me the directions."

"It's no problem. After what you've been through, you deserve a good night's rest. You can have the bed. I'll take the sofa," said Carol.

"No, you won't! I'm the one intruding. You've been more than kind," Margaret protested.

"I insist," returned Carol with a smile. Not waiting for Margaret's reply, she said good night, unfolded the sleeper sofa, and settled in.

"I don't think I'll be able to sleep anyway," said Margaret, heading for the small bedroom. How wrong she was, because the moment her head hit the pillow, she was sound asleep.

15

Soon morning arrived, and Margaret awakened with the sun streaming in through the window. The wonderful smell of coffee brewing was present throughout the small apartment. She opened her eyes and for a moment did not recognize her surroundings. She threw back the covers and looked around the room. She quietly got out of bed and headed for the area where she heard familiar sounds like those of a kitchen. It all started coming back to her slowly when she entered the small kitchen and saw Carol in the midst of making breakfast.

"Hello there," Carol said brightly, turning to look at her house guest. "Did you sleep well?" she asked.

"Yes, thanks. I didn't think I would, but I guess I was more tired than I thought," replied Margaret.

"You needed it. What do you have planned for today?" asked Carol.

"I guess I should be on my way," Margaret responded.

"On your way to where?" asked Carol.

Margaret gave no answer because she knew she had no place to go. After a while, she replied, "Thanks for everything, Carol. I don't know what I would have done without you."

"Don't mention it," Carol replied. "I hope if I were in your position, someone would do the same for me. Are you ready for breakfast?"

"Yes," replied Margaret. "I'm starving."

They enjoyed a hearty breakfast, and soon they were chatting like old friends. Margaret did the breakfast dishes and cleaned up the kitchen. It was the least she could do.

The dishes were stacked, and they were both enjoying a second cup of coffee when Carol asked. "Margaret, I've been thinking about this long and hard, and you don't have to give me an answer this minute. Anyway, why don't you stay here until you decide what you want to do? I know the apartment is small, but I don't mind if you don't, and I do enjoy the company."

Margaret looked at Carol with surprise. "I…I don't know what to say. I have next to no money…" she stammered, tears starting to well up in her eyes. "You've been so kind already, and you don't even know me. How could I ever repay you?"

"I don't expect repayment. It's the least I can do," Carol replied, smiling.

Margaret was quiet as she thought about the invitation that had just been ushered to her. *What do I have to lose?* she asked herself. She had never been shown such kindness since her aunt and uncle had taken her into their home. *I guess there are still kind people left in the world*, she thought. And so she decided to give this new town a try.

"I'll stay," she told Carol. "Just let me know when I start getting on your nerves."

They hugged each other warmly, and Carol hurried off to work.

Maybe my life will turn around in this new town. Thank you, God, for giving me a second chance. I don't intend to waste it.

"How do you feel about working in a diner?" Carol asked Margaret on her return from work a few days later.

"I don't know," replied Margaret. "I've never worked in one before. As a matter of fact, I've never had a job, but I'm sure I could learn. Do they have a vacancy?"

"Yes," replied Carol. "Lou, the owner, was just mentioning today that he needs some extra hands on board. They're constructing a new shopping mall not far from the diner, and the lunch rush is overwhelming. I told him I knew someone who might be interested. So if you're sure, he'll see you tomorrow if you have nothing planned."

"What could I have planned?" Margaret asked. "That sounds great. I've been calling a few places that I saw listed in the paper, but so far no one wants to hire a housewife with no work experience," she sighed.

Morning dawned bright and clear, and Margaret was up early and looking forward to her job interview. She tried tamping down her anxiety as she realized she had never been interviewed for a job before.

"How hard could it be," she asked herself. Carol had taken her shopping a few days before, so she was dressed in the only new outfit she had to her name. She and Carol wore the same size, so Carol had loaned her one of her fall coats. And so here she was, all snuggled up in Carol's coat, preparing for her first job interview.

Isn't life funny? she thought to herself. *Here I am going on my first job interview. If anyone had told me a few weeks ago that today I would be going for an interview in a different state, I would have called them a liar. God certainly works in mysterious ways.*

Finally, Carol finished dressing, and they left the apartment together; Carol to the daily grind of waitressing and Margaret to meet with Lou, the manager. Lou was a big burly hunk of a man who saw humor in just about everything. Even though she had no work experience, Lou loved Margaret on sight.

"All I need is someone who can take an order and deliver it to the right customer. If my customers are happy, they'll keep coming back, and that means money in my pocket. If there's money in my pocket, then you can afford to keep your job." He gave a hearty laugh at his own joke. "So you see, my dear, it's a win-win all around. Margaret, so far you seem to fit the bill, so you're hired."

Margaret was so happy she gave Lou a big hug. "Oh, thank you, thank you, Lou. I promise that I won't disappoint you."

Ever the businessman, Lou asked, "So can you start tomorrow?"

"But of course," she replied smilingly.

"Okay, I'll see you then. Carol will give you your uniform and fill you in about how the place runs."

And so Margaret started her new life as a waitress working at the Blue Bird Diner in Sycamore, Connecticut.

Soon two years had flown by, and Margaret had almost forgotten about her old life in Plains, New York. But Luke Foster had not forgotten!

16

As Luke's car careened around the curb, he could see Margaret's blue Toyota approaching the center of the drawbridge. He hit the accelerator and his car picked up speed. "You'll never get away from me, no matter how hard you try," he yelled out angrily. He knew she could not hear him, but he had to release the anger burning inside, or it would consume him.

He could see the drawbridge starting to separate, but he told himself he could make it across before it separated completely. He seemed mesmerized as he focused on Margaret's car, which appeared to be suspended in midair preparing to land on the other side. This just gave his anger an added surge of energy. Like a man possessed, he yelled, "I can make it across. Be prepared to meet your maker, Margaret."

Closer and closer he came, and with one final push to the accelerator, he was airborne—but too late; the bridge had already opened all the way. All he could do was grip the steering wheel as his car took a nosedive heading downward to the water below!

In his haste to block Margaret's escape, Luke had not taken the time to adequately secure his seat belt, and this would greatly contribute to his downfall. As his car hit the water, his anger reached boiling point. As a result, he forgot one cardinal rule: If you're involved in an accident and your vehicle is going off the road and into a body of water, adopt a brace position.

Too late!

On impact, Luke's chest slammed into the steering wheel; his head snapped backward, colliding with the head rest. The seat belt came undone, and with a great big whoosh, the airbag deployed, exploding into his face with considerable force. A cloud of fine white powder covered his entire face and chest. He was temporarily blinded by the powder and unaware of the tears flowing down his cheeks. His face felt like a thousand mosquitoes had descended and was feasting on his skin. He raised his hand to feel his face, but it was like fire to his touch. His last thought before descending into unconsciousness was *I need to live. If it's the last thing I do, I want to see her suffer. I can't let her get away with making me feel less than a man.*

The car floated down the river, but Luke was barely conscious. He was unaware of his dilemma as the motion of the water lulled him to sleep. He was in and out of consciousness, with no sense of time and no idea how long he had been in the water. The only thing he was aware of was that he could not move the lower portion of his body; all that was present was a profound sense of numbness.

By now the car had started tilting, the weight of the engine pulling it down into the water. As consciousness returned, he flailed around, trying to focus. During one episode of lucidity, he tried opening the driver's door, but it refused to budge. He tried recalling what he had heard about escaping from a car if you were trapped underwater, but it had all slipped his mind. Water entering the car was soon up to his knees.

Orientation returned for a while and, along with it, a feeling of desperation. Still intent on escaping his watery prison, he decided he would try to break the window. He made a fist and banged on the window in an attempt to break it but without success. He realized he needed a heavy object to do the job, but there was nothing within reach that he could use. Suddenly he remembered he had a toolbox on the backseat.

If I could only reach it, I could find something to break the window, he thought.

He reached out in an attempt to retrieve the toolbox, but in an instant, orientation deserted him, and he had no idea where the backseat was located. His breathing was now rapid and labored, his chest started to tighten, and his struggling increased. The water was now up to his chest, and he was still unable to move his legs. Soon the sunlight was completely obliterated, and he was surrounded by nothing but darkness. A new realization dawned on him—he was going to die!

His last thought before darkness descended was, *Please, God. I have never asked for anything before, but if you will just let me live, I promise I'll change.*

The car was now completely filled with water, and the final descent into oblivion was almost complete.

17

As the crowd on the bridge continued to grow, multiple calls were being placed to the 911 operator.

"911 operator, what is your emergency?"

"A car just went off the bridge," replied the caller anxiously.

"Which bridge is this, sir?" the operator asked.

"The Plains drawbridge. Hurry please," replied the anxious caller.

"Are you related to the person in the car?" asked the operator.

"No, I was waiting in line for the drawbridge to open when this car came sailing through the air and landed in the water. This person was pursuing another car."

"Did you say two cars went into the water, sir?" the operator asked anxiously.

"No…no. The first car was able to clear the drawbridge before it opened all the way, but the second car did not."

"Okay, sir. Emergency vehicles are on their way," replied the operator.

A small crowd had now gathered by the railing, and the sound of emergency vehicles could be heard getting closer and closer. Soon the area was a sea of emergency responders. They wasted no time getting into their gears and heading for the water to try and rescue Luke.

The first few dives were unsuccessful. The crowd looked on anxiously, holding their breath and hoping that each dive would be the last and that *the poor driver* would soon be *found*. Finally, his car was located, and the focus now centered on extricating him. Cheers went up from the crowd by the railing as a diver surfaced with a body in his arms. He was immediately joined by two EMTs, who proceeded to initiate rescue breathing. This was proving to be quite a challenge, but they never gave up.

The small group of rescuers proceeded to the riverbank, each one assisting with keeping his body in a prone position. They finally made it to the riverbank and placed him on a solid surface and continued their rescue efforts.

It was autumn, so the temperature of the water was almost at freezing point. It was therefore not surprising that his body temperature was extremely low, having been in the water for some time. Although he was completely unresponsive, the EMTs never assumed the worse and kept working to see if they could evoke a response.

"Check his airway," one EMT called out. The EMT standing by his head inserted a gloved finger into *his* mouth and moved it around, checking for any foreign material.

"Clear," he shouted. He was handed an oxygen mask, which he quickly applied over the patient's mouth and nose to provide much-needed oxygen to his lungs.

After a while, another EMT called out, "I have a heartbeat."

They quickly transferred *the unresponsive driver* onto a gurney then into the ambulance. His wet clothing was promptly removed, and he was wrapped in warm blankets for the short ride to Plains Medical Center.

The ER had been informed of their pending arrival, so no sooner had they arrived than the patient was whisked into one of the many cubicles. He was immediately surrounded by professionals all skilled in the art of lifesaving. So like a hive of busy worker bees, they all went about doing what they did best—saving lives. The first ER doctor inserted a tube into the patient's trachea while the respiratory therapist patiently waited to connect the tube to the breathing machine. Placing his stethoscope on the patient's chest, the doctor listened for breath sounds to ensure that the tube was in his lungs and not his stomach.

"It's in," he announced, removing the stethoscope from his ears. The tube was securely anchored in place with surgical tape to prevent it from being dislodged. The respiratory therapist quickly connected the tube to the machine then entered the prescribed settings on the respirator. As the respirator breathed for Luke, his chest rose and fell rhythmically with the machine, each precious breath supplying lifesaving oxygen into his lungs and vital organs.

At the same time, other teams were busy attaching electrodes to his chest to monitor his heart rate while others were cleaning his skin in preparation for obtaining blood specimens. While a catheter was being inserted into his bladder to monitor his urinary output, others were preparing to insert a central line into an artery to monitor his heart and deliver fluids.

"What's his name?" asked the doctor in charge. The EMTs had located his wallet with his driver's license, so at least he had a name and would not have to be referred to as "John Doe."

"Luke Foster," the EMT replied. "Any family members with him in the car?" the doctor asked. "No, sir, and no emergency contact listed either," replied the EMT.

His condition was determined to be critical, so as soon as he was stabilized, he was transferred to the Intensive Care Unit.

18

There is an old world phrase, "once a man, twice a child," and in his current condition, Luke Foster was living proof of this. Here he was, a grown man with no less than ten strangers observing him in all his nakedness. Had he been awake, it would have to be a cold day in the Sahara before he would allow complete strangers to encroach into his personal space. But life takes many strange twists and turns, and there are times when we have absolutely no power of control. This was one of those times.

For weeks, Luke remained unresponsive, totally dependent on the kindness of strangers. Machines were doing his breathing, tubes emptied his bladder, while another supplied his nutrition. All his needs were being met by people he did not know, but this was the hand he had been dealt, and he had no say in the matter. As much as he had enjoyed controlling the life of his wife, this was one situation that was entirely out of his control.

It is said that the sense of hearing is often present after all other senses have ceased to function, and so the staff treated Luke as if he was able to hear and understand.

A battery of tests had been done as soon as he had entered the ER. His initial chest x-rays had shown he had aspirated water into his lungs, so the onset of pneumonia was something to be expected in the near future. CT scans and MRIs of his brain had also shown extensive swelling, and the MRI of his spine had revealed an incomplete injury to his spinal cord.

Four weeks had now gone by since the accident, and Luke was finally starting to regain consciousness. The first indication was when he opened his eyes and stared blankly at his surroundings. Soon he would follow the nurse with his eyes as she moved around the room. The ICU staff was ecstatic to see that he was finally awake. Charles, the ICU Physician's assistant, was the happiest. He had spent many long hours day and night fighting to save Luke's life, and he was very happy to see the results of his hard work.

"Welcome back, Luke," he said, smiling and squeezing Luke's hand. "It's good to see you're awake. How are you feeling? Are you in pain?"

Luke just stared, making no response that he understood what was being asked. The tube was still in his airway, so even if he wanted to speak, it would have been impossible.

"Luke, you're back with us," said the nurse smilingly. Luke gave no response. Charles took a seat by Luke's bed and started asking him some questions. "Do you know where you are?" Charles asked. Luke shook his head no.

"Good, at least you're starting to understand," said Charles happily. Suddenly Luke started moving his arms in an attempt to remove the breathing tube. Charles quickly stood up and grabbed hold of one arm while the nurse held on to the other.

"Luke, the tube is there to help you breathe. If you remove it, you won't be able to breathe," the nurse explained, fighting to hold on to his arm. Luke fought back with superhuman strength. Despite the explanation, his anxiety continued to escalate. Fear was obvious in his eyes as he struggled to remove the tube.

"I'll have to give you some medicine to keep you calm, Luke. Until you're calm, we cannot remove the tube. Do you understand!" the PA yelled. Despite the constant reassurance, Luke did not appear to understand, and so he kept on fighting. The more the nurse and the PA struggled to keep his arms away from the tube, the more he fought.

"Luke, we'll have to restrain your arms. This is for your protection!" yelled Charles. The continuous blaring of both the respirator alarm and the cardiac monitor just added to the chaos. The commotion brought other staff members running to see what was going on. "Get some restraints!" Charles yelled to one of the nurses. She ran out and soon returned with restraints for all four limbs. After what seemed like a long and vigorous bout of wrestling, they finally got all four extremities safely anchored to the bed frame. However, this did nothing to reduce his struggling.

As the struggle escalated, so did his respiratory rate. His entire body was now awash with perspiration. Finally, Charles realized he had no option but to sedate him. He gave the order to one of the nurses, who dashed from the room to get the sedative. As soon as she returned, Charles administered the injection via the intravenous tubing, and as the medicine took effect, his heart rate slowly returned to normal and so did his breathing. Luke drifted off to sleep, bringing back some much-needed peace and quiet.

"I feel as if I just finished running a marathon," said one of the nurses, leaning against the wall, straightening her uniform while wiping perspiration from her face.

"Same here," replied Charles, bending forward, fighting to catch his breath.

To the uninformed bystander, the entire situation might seem like chaos at its highest level, but as the saying goes, sometimes out of chaos comes order. The staff gradually drifted off to other assignments, happy this much-needed order had returned.

But for how long?

19

Luke was now kept sedated for his own safety. The restraints were removed from his extremities at frequent intervals and the area massaged to ensure that his circulation was not compromised. However, the moment he woke up, the fight would begin again. This went on for another week, until finally he was calm enough for a respiratory trial to see if he could breathe on his own.

The first time the tracheal tube was disconnected from the breathing machine, he was able to tolerate its removal for only a few minutes. The process was repeated daily, and each time he was able to tolerate it for longer periods without going into respiratory distress.

The day finally arrived for the breathing tube to be completely removed. Everyone hoped that Luke would achieve complete success by breathing completely on his own. The respiratory therapist, Charles, and Luke's assigned nurse gathered at his bedside.

"Luke, you have done so well without the breathing tube we're going to remove it for good. I want you to take some deep, slow breaths. Do you understand?" asked Charles.

Luke nodded yes. A syringe was used to deflate the balloon holding the tube in place, and Luke was asked to take a deep breath. He was gently suctioned and the tube slowly withdrawn. The moment the tip of the catheter emerged, he was racked by a violent episode of coughing. Suctioning was repeated and all the excess secretions removed.

"Slow down, Luke. Take some deep breaths," Charles quietly reassured him. Eventually, his breathing slowed to a regular rate, and an oxygen mask was placed over his nose and mouth. This was a lot more comfortable than the tube in his airway, but the tube had left his throat quite sore. He struggled to speak, but his voice came out only as a hoarse croak. The frustration he was feeling was visible all over his face as he fought to be understood.

"Don't struggle, Luke. We'll have to put you back on the machine if you don't calm down," Charles cautioned him. Luke seemed to take him at his word and did his best to calm down.

To assist with his reorientation, the nurse gave him a pen and paper to communicate. "Luke, it will be difficult for you to speak right away because you've had the tube in your throat for a long time. You need to rest your voice and be patient. Whatever you need to say, just write it on this paper."

For some individuals, the actual illness or injury they sustain can cause them to feel confused, disorientated, anxious, or frightened. This was now the case with Luke. The following days he spent sitting out of bed, staring at his surroundings, trying to determine where he was. Soon his voice, which started out as hoarse and guttural, gradually returned to normal.

His first words were, "Where am I?" His voice was full of fear and his eyes filled with terror as he realized he was unable to move his legs. He kept looking around, frightened at the unfamiliar surroundings. Nothing he saw he recognized.

"What happened to my legs?" he asked fearfully.

"Do you remember the accident, Luke?" asked the nurse.

"What accident?" he asked. "I don't remember an accident. Was anyone hurt?" he asked, his voice rising.

"No. You were the only one in the car," replied the nurse.

"I can't remember. Can you please help me remember?" he pleaded with tears in his eyes.

"Give yourself time, Luke. Your memory will come back," said the nurse, patting him on the back sympathetically.

Luke felt like a stranger in a strange land. He could not remember his name or where he lived. He answered to "Luke" or "Mr. Foster" because he thought that must be his name; otherwise, why would they refer to him as such? To make matters worse, he had lost control of his bowel and bladder functions and was totally dependent on the nursing staff. His embarrassment was so acute he could not hold back the tears whenever they cared for him.

He was filled with helplessness and shame. "I'm so sorry," he would say to the staff. "I'm a man, this should not be happening to me. I'm so sorry."

"Don't worry, Luke. It's not your fault. Just try focusing on getting better," they responded kindly.

Dr. Wong, the neurologist, paid Luke one of his regular visits and discussed the results of his tests. "Your recent brain MRI shows signs of great improvement, Luke. Your blood tests have ruled out chemical imbalances, and everything neurological seems to be coming along just fine." Overall, the news was very encouraging, but Luke received the news with guarded optimism.

"I'm going to transfer you to a bed on the rehab floor, Luke. You'll be starting on a regimen of physiotherapy that will help to strengthen your lower limbs. It will go a long way toward helping you regain your strength and get you walking again. I have also ordered speech and occupational therapy to help with your memory," Dr. Wong told him.

"Are you sure they can help me, Doctor?" Luke asked skeptically.

"Just be patient and cooperate with the staff. This will not happen overnight, but it will happen," the doctor encouraged.

And so Luke continued his struggle, trying to remember who he was, what had caused the accident, and what his past life had been like.

⁂

The following morning, Luke was transferred from the ICU to the rehab unit. He missed the ICU staff and his single room as he now had to share a room with another patient. *It's so much quieter than the ICU*, he thought to himself. *At least I'll be able to hear myself think.*

Later in the day, he met with the physiotherapist and the occupational therapist to discuss the details of his therapy. "You'll start your exercises daily for the first week, and then based on your progress, we'll increase it to twice daily," the therapist told him. "We'll vary the exercises to see how well you tolerate them. After that, we'll gradually increase the frequency and intensity as well as the duration."

"I'm anxious to get out of here," he replied. "So I'll do my best."

"Remember, Luke, there are some things you can't hurry. I've seen patients try to overdo their exercises, and in the end, it just caused more harm. There are some things in life you can't hurry—the healing process is one of them."

Soon he was able to transfer into his wheelchair without assistance, and as soon as this happened, Luke was in no mood for taking it slow. Quite often, he could be found in the physiotherapy room. At times he was so discouraged he felt like quitting, but a small part of his brain kept telling him to keep going.

I want to know who I was before all this happened, he told himself.

With that thought in mind, he would double his efforts to work on his exercises. Some days he was so driven he would work himself almost to the point of exhaustion. At these times, his body would scream for pain relief, but he was in no mood to listen, so he chose to ignore it and kept on going.

"Don't overdo it, Luke," the physiotherapist warned him. "You'll only do more harm than good." But Luke was in no mood to listen to reason.

"I want to get out of here," he responded.

"I understand, but you can't hurry time," the therapist would reply.

20

It was now two months since Luke was admitted to Plains Hospital, but despite the aggressive therapy, he was barely able to ambulate on his own. He had regained some sensation in his legs and was now able to move his toes. His memory was slowly returning, and he could recall small incidents that occurred before the accident, but not the accident itself. He could not recall his marriage to Margaret, where he lived, or the type of work he once did. To make matters worse, he had had no visitors during all the time he was hospitalized. It was as if he didn't exist before the accident. His lack of visitors seemed unusual to the staff but not totally unheard of. Intervention from Social Services was requested, but try as they might, they could not locate any of his relatives.

Ms. Ramirez was the social worker assigned to his case. She had visited with him on more than one occasion but had no good news to deliver. Today another meeting was scheduled, and she was ambivalent about the meeting. She was not quite sure if his usual bad mood was due to his accident, his current condition, or just a matter of clashing personalities. She did not reveal his mood swings to the rest of the rehab team but wanted to observe his behavior a while longer.

When she arrived, Luke was sitting quietly in his wheelchair in a corner of the therapy area. One look at him told her he was in one of his bad moods. She greeted him politely but received no response.

"Mr. Foster, I have no good news for you today as far as locating your relatives, but I haven't given up," she began. "It's been four months now, and my main concern is having some type of support system in place for you when you leave here."

"I don't need anyone. I'll be able to take care of myself as soon as I get out of this chair. I just want to remember who I was before this happened, then get out of this place," he replied angrily.

Ms. Ramirez was not surprised at the hostility in his voice. "Are you able to recall anything about yourself before the accident, Mr. Foster?" asked Ms. Ramirez.

"If I was able to, don't you think I'd tell you?" he replied.

Realizing she would not get any useful information from him, Ms. Ramirez collected her file and stood to go. "Mr. Foster, when you're ready for me to help you, let me know." With that, she rose and headed for the door.

Luke continued with his rehabilitation, doing additional hours despite being cautioned by the rehab team to take it slower. His mood swings was now the talk of the entire unit, and although he was pleasant the majority of the time, his behavior was enough to deter more than a few of the therapists.

"You're making very good progress, Luke," Dr. Sanford told him at the regular rehab patient conference.

"Yes, but not fast enough," he responded.

"Well, I have some news I hope you'll like," the doctor continued. "Our work with you here is done, and you're now ready for transfer to another rehab facility. At this facility, the staff will continue working with you to restore you to your best optimal health. We've done all we can for you here, so this will be the next phase in your recuperation process," replied Dr. Sanford.

"Why can't I stay here and finish my treatment?" Luke asked.

"Well, the acute phase of your care is now over, and it's time to focus on trying to fix the other areas. The Carlton Rehab has specialists who can deal with these different areas of your care. They'll do a more intense course of therapy that we're not equipped to do here. You'll like it there. I hear they call it the Ritz Carlton, it's so glamorous," laughed Dr. Sanford.

"I hope so. When do I leave?" Luke asked.

"Well, consider this your lucky day. I know it's short notice, but they have a bed available for you tomorrow. The Carlton Rehab Center is well known for their care of patients suffering from the type of injury you sustained. They usually have a very long waiting list, so we were really lucky to get you in at such short notice. I know you'll love it there."

"I hope so," Luke replied.

The conference ended, and Luke sat and pondered about what he had just been told. Unknown to the staff, pieces of his old life had started to flash across his memory, but they were so vague and fleeting he did not recognize them. As the days had progressed, more and more of the staff had started noticing that his mood swings were becoming more frequent. They had discussed it among themselves and decided they would continue to observe him. However, now that he was ready for discharge, they hoped he would get over it or be open for some kind of intervention.

"I hope this new place can make me better. I hate having to depend on someone to take care of me, and I'm tired of sitting in this wheelchair," he said angrily as he wheeled himself back to his room. That night he fell asleep and for the first time dreamed about being married to a beautiful girl he met in high school.

21

The next day dawned bright and sunny, and Luke awakened with a sense of expectancy. He rolled over and transferred into his wheelchair. He suddenly remembered that he would be transferring to the rehab center that day, so he started gathering his few belongings. Suddenly he stopped what he was doing as he had a flash of memory.

"That was a weird dream I had last night!" he said to himself.

"What was that, Luke?" asked Cindy the therapist who had just walked into the room.

Luke smiled at her. "I had this dream last night that I was married to a beautiful girl. My high school sweetheart it seemed like." Suddenly the smile was replaced by a frown.

"Who would want to marry me anyway? Even if I had a wife, she wouldn't want me back now. Look at me, I can't even walk. Nobody would want me. Furthermore, if this were true, she would have come to visit me."

Cindy could not help but feel sympathy toward him although she didn't know if this was the real Luke or not. He was such a complex person; it was difficult to really get to know the real Luke. After listening to him unburden himself, Cindy thought to herself, *It must be difficult not remembering anything about your past.* However, she knew Luke could be very manipulative, and she really had no plans to join him on his little journey of self-pity.

"Stop feeling sorry for yourself, Luke. You'll get your memory back, and when you do, you'll work it out. You're a handsome young man. I'm sure there are quite a number of beautiful girls waiting for you out there somewhere," said Cindy.

Luke made no reply as she turned and headed for the door. Before she reached the door, Luke called out to her. "Excuse me, Cindy. Can you stay for a while?"

"Okay, but not for long though. I have some reports I must finish today." She stood next to him, waiting for him to say what was on his mind. "So what's on your mind?" she asked after a deafening pause.

Luke fumbled as if embarrassed but finally said what he was thinking. "I know this might sound a bit unexpected, and I probably shouldn't ask, but could you come and visit me at the rehab center? I don't seem to have any family, so…" he hesitated. "If you would come to visit me, I'd really appreciate it."

Having said what was on his mind, he could not bring himself to look Cindy in the eye, so he kept his head down as he fumbled with the handles of his wheelchair.

Cindy was taken by surprise at the request but tried her best to cover it up. She had never given him any reason to come on to her, and he had never before shown any interest in her. *Maybe this is just a friendly gesture. I don't want to get involved with a patient, especially not Luke. He's much too moody for my taste*, she thought to herself.

"Oh, Luke," she said enthusiastically. "That's so nice of you to ask. Of course, I'll come. You don't have to be embarrassed. As soon as you're settled in, I'll check to see when visiting hours are scheduled, and I'll come see you."

"Thanks, Cindy. For a minute, I thought you were going to say no. I guess I'll see you then."

She smiled and continued out the door. "Bye, Luke. Take care of yourself, and do what they tell you, okay?"

"I'll try," Luke replied.

At ten o'clock, the ambulette arrived to take Luke to the Carlton Rehabilitation Center in the nearby town of New Hope. It was located only a short distance from the hospital, and within thirty minutes they arrived. On entering the gates of the center, Luke stared in awe at the magnificent structure in front of him. It towered to a height of over twenty stories, and the sunlight reflecting off the windows looked like millions of tiny rainbows. The building was surrounded by beautiful eye-catching landscape that seemed to stretch for miles.

To complete the scenery, there was a cascading waterfall, which added just the right touch of elegance, and the cool, clear water seemed to be flowing down from some natural unseen source.

"Wow, this must be what heaven looks like! No wonder they call it the 'Ritz.' I'm not sure what the name means, but it sure sounds rich. A place like this must cost a lot of money," Luke murmured.

"Don't worry man," the transport aide replied. "I'm sure you have very good insurance. They'll pay for all of this. If you had to pay out of your pocket…" He laughed and left the sentence hanging as he proceeded to the admissions desk.

Luke could not help but notice; in fact, anyone who was not visually impaired could not help but notice the tastefully decorated foyer. Magnificent paintings were mounted on the walls while large potted plants were strategically placed in all the right locations.

Luke continued looking on in awe as he was wheeled to the elevator and whisked to his room on the sixth floor. He was met by Sophie the head nurse and Randy the chief therapist. His room was so clean and spacious, he felt like he was in a five-star hotel. Soon he was settled in, and it seemed as if he had lived there all his life.

The next day, he started on a vigorous schedule of physical and occupational therapy, and as much as he enjoyed the "Ritz," he also looked forward to returning to his normal life, whatever "normal" was.

22

Life at the rehab center was anything but boring. The schedule was backbreaking, and at times Luke thought he would never make it, but he told himself he could not afford to give up. The atmosphere was pleasant and informal, and the staff all insisted they be called by their first name. In addition to the daily rigors of therapy, the patients were entertained with weekly concerts, movie nights, and ice cream socials. Overall it didn't feel like a hospital but more like a high-end hotel. In no time, a month had gone by, and Luke continued to enjoy all the amenities of the Ritz.

Life is good, he thought to himself. *What makes it even better is that Cindy's coming to visit me today.* He could not wait for her to arrive. She had visited him a few times before and somehow had talked himself into believing that Cindy was developing more than friendly feelings toward him.

Soon it was visiting time, and as Cindy headed toward the visitors' lounge, she decided not to put it off any longer. "I think today is as good a day as any," she said to herself. "I just want to get this out of the way and get on with our friendship."

Luke was waiting when she arrived and greeted her effusively.

"Let's go out on the balcony. It's nice and quiet out there, the scenery is beautiful, and we can talk without anyone eavesdropping," he said happily as he led the way to the balcony.

Cindy held the door open, making it easier for him to navigate his wheelchair. "You're in such a good mood today, Luke," said Cindy.

"Yes, I am," Luke replied. "There's something I want to ask you. When you hear it, you'll be just as happy as I am," He smiled at Cindy.

Cindy's heart skipped a beat, hoping against hope that it was not what she suspected. If it was, then she would have to turn him down gently because what she felt for him was nothing beyond friendship. She sincerely hoped he would understand. "I have something to tell you too," said Cindy. "How about if I go first?"

"Okay, shoot," Luke replied.

Cindy started feeling nervous. *This is so much harder than I thought it would be,* she thought. She valued his friendship, and the last thing she wanted was to hurt his feelings, so she struggled to find the best way to approach this delicate subject.

"Luke," she began nervously. "I'm not sure how to say this, but I think I need to clear the air. You are a good friend, and I like you very much, but on my last visit, I got the feeling that you were thinking there was more to our friendship than there actually is. I need you to understand that there can be nothing between us but friendship. I hope I'm wrong about this and hope that we can continue to be friends." She paused and waited for his response.

Luke opened his mouth in surprise. This was not what he expected! He had often imagined that the relationship with Cindy was progressing well and that there might be a future for them both. And that was when the dark side that had been buried at the accident once more rose to the surface in full force.

Cindy could see his features starting to change. His neck veins started to bulge, his face reddened, and his pupils began to dilate as his rage mounted. She suddenly felt very afraid and started gathering her belongings to leave.

In a flash, he blocked the door with his wheelchair and turned to face Cindy. With his deep blue penetrating eyes, he slowly rolled toward her. Cindy quickly retreated into a corner, cowering like a frightened child. Luke growled as he approached her. "So you have been leading me on all this time? Is this how you treat someone who cares about you? You women are all alike. I should have known you were no different. Get out, and don't ever come back. Imagine I was thinking of asking you to marry me?"

He wheeled his chair toward the door, quickly threw it open, and rolled down the hallway without a backward glance. Frightened more than she could ever believe, Cindy grabbed her bag and beat a hasty retreat toward the exit as if her life depended on it.

Soon Luke was able to walk on his own, but with only a slight limp. He rarely ever needed assistance. The staff was proud of his progress and was glad to see him gain more independence daily. From his conversations, the staff realized that some areas of his memory had returned, but he still had difficulty with his long-term memory. Even though he got a bit morose at times, he was mostly in good spirits and pleasant to be around. He was in great spirits when he received the good news that he would be discharged home soon and couldn't wait to get going. He didn't know where "home" was going to be, but for some odd reason, he felt driven as if there was some task waiting for him to complete.

He had spent a full three months at the "Ritz," and at last, the day of discharge arrived, and all the staff had gathered to see him off. Spring was in the air, making his spirits lift even higher. Seeing the crowd gathered to wish him good luck, Luke felt like a rock star as he hugged each one good-bye and accepted their good wishes.

"Luke, you'll still need to continue therapy for your memory loss," Dr. Stone, his doctor, told him. "So make sure to keep your appointments."

"Sure, Doc. I won't forget." Luke hugged him hard, trying his best not to start blubbering like a little kid. "Thanks for everything, Doc."

He walked down the line hugging each staff member, trying hard not to cry, a task that was proving to be quite difficult. "Good-bye, everyone. Thanks for everything."

"I hope everything works out for you, Luke. Good luck," they all called out.

Luke almost ran into the taxi that had been arranged to take him to temporary housing. As he started down the drive, he waved until the cab turned a corner, and the staff were soon lost from view. Tears gathered in his eyes at the loss of his "family." After all, this was the closest that he could remember to having a real family.

23

"You okay, buddy?" asked the cab driver.

"Yes, I am," Luke replied. He sighed deeply. "It's just that I've been here for the past three months, and everyone has been so good to me. And now I have no idea what lies ahead."

"Don't you have any family?" asked the cabbie, staring at Luke through the rearview mirror.

"I don't remember," said Luke. "I was in an accident, and I can't remember what happened."

"You can't remember anything at all?" the cabbie asked, surprise audible in his voice.

Luke squirmed in his seat. "Not much, just little flashes here and there. I'm hoping I'll remember something before too long."

"Well, I'm sure your memory will come back in time. I hear they have lots of medical things to help you these days. I personally don't believe in doctors poking around in my brain…"

As the cabbie rambled on, Luke quickly lost interest and focused on the passing scenery. Nothing seemed familiar to him. No landmarks, no parks; not even a restaurant seemed familiar. It was all foreign land. For all he knew, he could be in Siberia.

"Here we are, buddy," the cabbie said, breaking into Luke's thoughts. "Good luck. I hope you remember something soon."

"Thanks," said Luke, paying the cabbie from the small amount of money they had given him at the rehab center. He didn't have much personal property, so he held on to the plastic bag, which held all his earthly possessions. It was spring, and the air was a bit nippy, so he wrapped his light coat around him and stood for a moment observing his new neighborhood. Standing on the sidewalk looking up at the building that was supposed to be his temporary home, he wondered how long he would have to live there. "This definitely would not have been my first choice, but beggars can't be choosers, I guess," he said to himself.

From where he stood, the neighborhood was far from desirable. In fact, it looked downright seedy. Quite a number of buildings were covered with graffiti. Paper and plastic bags, empty cans, bottles, and paper littered the sidewalk. Looking up and down the street, he continued to take stock of his new environment.

"Looks like someone had a bad aim," he said to himself, noticing the collection of trash scattered around the empty garbage container at the entrance to the building. The few trees that lined the street appeared stunted and seemed to be fighting desperately for their lives.

"Summer is almost here," Luke said to himself. "I'm sure when the flowers start blooming, it will look much better."

Luke reluctantly climbed the steps and entered the lobby of the building. He hoped his room would not be a reflection of what he had just seen outside. Entering the sparsely furnished lobby, he saw an older African American gentleman seated behind a desk. Luke stood for a while, sizing up the old man. Thinking he did not appear to be a threat, he finally approached the desk. He had been instructed to ask for the manager.

"Hi. I'm Luke Foster. I was told to ask for Mr. Saunders, the manager."

"Who told you to ask?" came the gruff reply.

"Ms. Adams," Luke replied.

"Sorry, I don't know anyone by that name."

Luke's heart sank at the thought of not having a place to stay in this strange neighborhood. He fumbled in his pocket and brought out a wrinkled piece of paper. With trembling hands, he handed it to the man at the desk. "Ms. Adams, the social worker at Carlton Rehab sent me. She told me that I would be staying here for a while."

The man took the paper, glanced at it, then looked up at Luke with a smile. "Well, why didn't you say that, son? I'm Mr. Saunders, the manager. I was just pulling your chain. Come with me, I'll show you to your room."

Luke took a deep breath, relief flooding over him. The man groaned, holding on to his back as he got up from behind the desk. He picked up a bunch of keys and beckoned for Luke to follow. As he followed, Luke noticed they were heading for the stairs. "Isn't there an elevator in the building?" Luke asked, looking apprehensively at the stairs. "Yes, but it's not working. The repairman should have been here yesterday, but he called to say he had an emergency. He should be here sometime today…hopefully." The last word he said softly under his breath.

As they climbed the stairs, Mr. Saunders kept up a steady stream of conversation. Luke listened but did not reply as he needed all his energy to focus on maneuvering up the stairs. They had taught him stair climbing while in rehab, but this definitely felt different!

"I'm sorry, young man. Ms. Adams did ask for a room on the first floor, and I promised her that I would have one. However, the gentleman in room 102 was supposed to move out today, but unfortunately he did not. He will be leaving tomorrow though, so I want you to stay in this room tonight, then tomorrow you can move into that room. I know the stairs are difficult for you, but it's only for one night." Mr. Saunders kept walking up the stairs until he reached room 310.

"Here we are, young man. You'll be staying in this room tonight." Receiving no response, he turned to take a look, but

Luke was nowhere in sight. Mr. Saunders started back down the stairs, thinking something must have happened to his new tenant. Halfway down, he saw Luke leaning against the rails. He had had no choice but to stop and try to catch his breath.

Mr. Saunders took one look at him and could not help but laugh. "I'm sorry, young man. I didn't mean to leave you behind, but sometimes I just talk too much. My wife tells me that all the time. I talk and talk and don't wait for an answer. Anyway, as I was saying, tomorrow I will put you in the room on the first floor, so don't unpack all your stuff."

Realizing he had not seen any luggage accompanying Luke, he gave him a questioning look. "By the way son, where is your stuff?"

Luke had finally conquered the last step and was gradually regaining his breath. "Oh, I don't have much," he said, still breathing hard. "I plan to shop for some things as soon as I get settled. By the way, where is the nearest mall around here?" Looking through the window, Mr. Saunders pointed in an easterly direction.

"Not too far from here. Just go down one block, make a right, then go down another block, and it's right there."

"Thank you, Mr. Saunders," Luke replied. He accepted the keys and entered the room where he would be spending his first night out of rehab.

24

Luke spent a very restful first night. He slept better than he thought he would and was feeling very pleased with his new accommodations. After lunch he moved to the first floor where he would be spending the next few months. The room came already furnished, and he loved everything about it; in fact, he was surprised that it was so clean and spacious. In addition to a bedroom and a full bathroom, he also had a small sitting area where he could watch television and entertain, in case he had guests. There was also a kitchenette with a small fridge and even a microwave. "Not that I'll be doing much cooking," he smiled to himself. "I guess you should never judge a book by its cover," he continued, remembering his first impression of the building's exterior.

This is the first time since the accident that I feel a sense of independence, he thought to himself as he moved from room to room. *However, I better not get too attached to this place. This is only a temporary stop.* He spent a very restful night with no dreams to interrupt his sleep. He soon settled in comfortably and in no time was familiar with his new neighborhood. He made some new friends and started his commute twice weekly to the rehab center. He continued working hard at regaining full strength to his legs and was soon able to get around well without the aid of a cane. In fact, the only time he used it was when he wanted to gain sympathy from a beautiful girl.

Time flew by, and today for his appointment, he was stylishly dressed in dark-blue jeans and a light-blue shirt with the sleeves partially rolled up. An expensive-looking pair of loafers completed his ensemble. His dark hair was well combed, and his face was clean-shaven except for a small goatee. The distinct smell of expensive cologne was detectable when he entered the room.

Nancy, his regular therapist, was waiting to conduct his therapy session. She looked up from her paperwork as he entered and was surprised at the person standing before her. "Hi, Luke. You really look nice today. I hardly recognized you," she said, smiling.

"Well, I have another appointment when I'm finished here, so I wanted to look nice. I wanted to look nice for you too. Please don't misunderstand," he replied, smiling.

"That's great. It seems as if things are working out for you."

"You could say that," he replied. He took a seat in the vacant chair and made himself comfortable.

After getting the small talk out of the way, the session got underway. "Okay, let's get started. We have a lot of ground to cover. So far, your legs seem to be working quite well. Are there any problems with ambulating?" asked Nancy.

"No, no problems at all," replied Luke.

"Okay," Nancy responded. "Depending on your progress, we should be looking at a discharge from the rehab program in about two weeks. How does that make you feel?"

Luke squirmed in his seat as he tried coming up with an answer.

"Well…if that's what it has to be, then I have no choice but to go along with it," he finally replied.

"So how about your memory? Are you starting to remember more about your life before the accident?" asked Nancy.

"I'm starting to remember a few things," he replied nonchalantly.

"What things? Give me an example," Nancy prompted.

"Well, occasionally I have what seems like flashbacks, but I'm really not sure if it's a part of my past life or not. The other day I thought I remembered getting married right after high school, but I couldn't remember my wife's name, or if I had any kids."

Nancy noted that his body language seemed to speak a world of difference between what he was saying and what he was not. The fact that he refused to make eye contact with her spoke volumes. She sensed that he was not being forthright with her, so she remained quiet and continued to observe him.

"Maybe we should try hypnosis," Nancy finally suggested. "It's a well-known fact that it has helped many people to explore painful memories and feelings that are sometimes hidden from their conscious minds. These feelings are sometimes so painful that they're unaware that they may be blocking them. It could help to at least recall your wife's name."

The statement seemed to awaken something dormant within Luke. The muscles in his cheeks started to twitch, and his face reddened with suffused anger. Rising from his chair, he locked eyes with Nancy. "I said I don't remember her name, didn't you get that? Do you want me to lie to you?" he asked angrily.

The change was so sudden it took Nancy completely by surprise. She cowered in her chair. It was as if she was seeing this person for the first time. For a moment, she thought he was about to hit her as he kept clenching and unclenching his fist. As if in answer to her silent prayer, the door opened, and Karen, another therapist, walked in.

"Hi, Nancy. Hi, Luke," she said laughingly as she headed over to hug Luke. "It's so good to see you, Luke. You look very nice. How are things going? I guess I really don't have to ask," she said, smiling.

Luke tore his attention away from Nancy and looked up at Karen with a big smile on his handsome face. He moved toward her, hugged her hard, and then held her at arm's length. All the while his eyes roamed over her body, undressing her with his eyes. He finally released her.

"Things are going just fine, Karen. How are you? As beautiful as ever, eh?" he said with a wink. Karen was embarrassed by his open flirting. The last thing she wanted was to give him the wrong impression, so she asked worriedly, "I hope I didn't interrupt your session?" Luke made no reply.

Seeing the opportunity to escape, Nancy quickly seized it. She quietly got out from her chair and hurried from the room. Luke and Karen heard the door slam and were just in time to see Nancy hurrying out the door.

"Oh no," Luke replied. "We were just about finished anyway. I was getting a bit tired, so I was glad when you showed up to save the day," he said, giving her another one of his drop-dead smiles.

"I'd better go find Nancy and apologize for intruding on her session," said Karen worriedly, heading for the door.

"Oh, I'm sure she won't mind. Anyway, I have another appointment, so I'd better be on my way. I hope I get to see you next time I'm here."

"I hope so too," replied Karen brightly. However, the smile on her face was not reflected in her eyes. Together they headed out the door; Luke to keep his appointment and Karen to find Nancy and apologize.

This was one of Luke's many appointments with the social worker, and he was in no mood to listen to her harp on the subject of him finding a job.

"You need to find a job, Luke," he mimicked her as he headed toward her office. "If you don't find a job soon, we'll be forced to stop payments on your apartment," he continued mimicking.

"I'm so sick of hearing that," he said to himself. As he knocked on her door, he could feel his anger starting to build.

"Who is it?" a voice from the office called out.

"It's Luke, Ms. Adams. I have an appointment with you."

"Oh, yes. Come on in, Luke," came the response.

Luke pushed open the door and, without acknowledging the social worker, took a seat in the only vacant chair. Ms. Adams reached out to shake his hand, but Luke refused to acknowledge the gesture.

"Well," said Ms. Adams, fighting hard to control her voice. "Good morning to you too, Mr. Foster."

Again Luke refused to answer. Locating his records, she turned the pages until she found what she needed.

"So how are you doing?" she asked.

Still no response.

"Okay," said Ms. Adams, still fighting to remain professional. "So tell me, Luke. Have you been able to find a job?"

Luke tilted his head to one side and stared at the ceiling, trying hard to control his anger. Regaining a semblance of control, he faced the social worker, unsmiling. "How do you expect me to find a job when I have no college degree?" he asked.

Taking a deep breath, Ms. Adams replied, "On your last visit, I gave you a list of companies that were hiring. These jobs did not require that you have a college degree. Did you visit any of those companies?" she asked in desperation.

Luke gave her a look full of pure hatred before slowly getting out of his chair. "You know what, Ms. Adams? I don't want those menial jobs. They don't pay enough money, and I need a lot of money real fast. I need to find my wife. She's the reason I'm in this mess. I used to have a nice job and a nice apartment, and she's the reason for my losing everything. If it's the last thing I do, I'm going to find her and make her pay." He banged his fist on the desk, causing Ms. Adams to jump.

Ms. Adams blinked, not believing what she had just heard. "So I see your memory has returned? How long has this been, Luke?" she asked.

"That is none of your business!" he snapped.

"It is my business," she replied. "I have to document everything that takes place during your visits. Failure to do so would be failure to do my job. I have to inform the chief and the rest of the team that your memory has returned."

Realizing what this could mean for him, he quickly asked, "What does this mean in terms of my room and allowance?"

"Well, there will be a meeting with the team, and depending on the findings, a decision will be made. If it's determined that you are fully capable of providing for yourself, you will be discharged from the program, and we will no longer be responsible for you. In the meantime, I strongly suggest that you find a job. I'll be in touch, Luke."

Ms. Adams gathered her paperwork then stood up, indicating that the meeting was over. Luke knew he had been caught in his own lie, and he was now at the end of this road. However, he was determined not to go out looking like a chump, so he slowly stood up, and with both hands resting on the desk, he bent forward just inches from the social worker's face. Making sure he had eye contact, he glared menacingly at her. He raised his hand as if to strike. Ms. Adams sat quietly back in her chair and watched as in a trance.

"You'd better make sure that whatever happens in this room today stays in this room. If not, you'll be hearing from me," he said. Seeing that no response was forthcoming, he straightened his shoulders, smiled, then turned and walked out the door. Ms. Adams slowly released a breath, her heart feeling as if it was about to burst from her chest. It took a while for her to recover from her encounter with Luke, but as soon as she did, she called and scheduled a meeting with the rehab team for the next day.

25

Early the following morning, all members of the physical and occupational therapy departments, the psychologist, neurologist, nursing staff, and social services were present and on time. After greeting everyone, Dr. Stone, the rehab chief, opened the meeting. He looked around the table then at Ms. Adams. "Let's get started. Ms. Adams. Why don't you start, seeing you're the one who called this meeting?"

Ms. Adams opened her binder, and the meeting got underway. Everyone stared in rapt attention. "I had a meeting with Luke Foster yesterday, and he apparently had a slip of the tongue," she began. "He has been hiding the fact that his memory has completely returned. How long it has returned, I have no idea. However, he has refused to look for a job, even though I have given him a list of jobs that were available. What surprised me more than anything was the reason he gave for needing more money."

"What was the reason?" asked Dr. Stone.

"He claimed he wanted to find his wife and let her pay for what she has done to him," Ms. Adams replied. A quick intake of breath was all that could be heard at the table as each person looked from one to the other.

"Did he say what she had done?" asked Dr. Stone.

"He claimed she had taken everything away from him and that he would find her and make her pay. But what really scared me was the way he acted. When I asked if he had gone to any of the jobs that I had recommended, you could see the rage in his eyes. To be honest, for a minute I was afraid to be in the same room with him."

Suddenly Nancy jumped as if scared. "Oh my goodness, I experienced the same thing with him myself," she said, looking frightened.

"What brought on this anger?' asked Dr. Stone, looking at Nancy.

"I asked him if his memory was returning and if he could remember anything about his wife. I thought he was going to hit me. Luckily, Karen came into the room. I left as fast as I could. I was so scared."

"Has anyone else experienced this type of reaction or anything similar from him?" asked Dr. Stone, looking around the table. An excited buzz started to circulate around the table. It was evident that other altercations had occurred that had not been brought to light. Dr. Stone rapped on the table for attention as all eyes seem to focus on Nancy.

"Nancy, is there anything you'd like to share?" he asked. Nancy nodded yes before starting to speak. "Does everyone remember Luke's friend Cindy? She used to visit him when he was first transferred here?" she asked. A few heads nodded while others focused on trying to recall Luke's visitor.

"Yes, I noticed she suddenly stopped coming. I was wondering why," said one therapist.

"Well," Nancy continued. "Cindy and I got to be friends. She's also a therapist at Plains Hospital, where Luke was staying before transferring to us. We were talking casually one day, and I asked why she had stopped visiting Luke. She told me Luke had misunderstood their relationship, and she had tried explaining to him that they could only be friends. She said she saw a side of him that scared her to the point that she never wanted to see him again. That's why she stopped coming."

"What did he do?" asked Dr. Wong.

"She said it was not a matter of what he did, but what he said, and the way he said it. She said she feared for her life. That's the way I felt yesterday. I was so glad when Karen walked into the room."

"I'm starting to see a picture of a very manipulative person who has taken advantage of our services. From what I've heard today, apparently his memory has returned for some time now, yet he has continued to act as if it had not. How could I not have seen it?" Dr. Stone asked himself. "When do you meet with him again, Ms. Adams?" he asked.

"I told him I would be in touch, but he threatened me before he left, so I'm not sure if I'll be seeing him again." she replied. Before adjourning, Dr. Wong gave one final piece of advice.

"In case anyone sees Luke, please be careful and notify security immediately. I'll be sure to give them a call myself to put them on alert. Thanks, everyone. Meeting adjourned."

As they dispersed, Nancy decided to visit the cafeteria before returning to her office. Karen hurried and caught up with her just before she entered the elevator. "Hey, Nancy. Can I have a word?" Karen called out.

"Sure. I'm going to the cafeteria. Want to come?" Nancy replied, slowing her pace.

"Why not?" replied Karen. "I brought my lunch, but I can always save it for tomorrow."

As usual, the elevator was crowded with both employees and visitors. They had to literally hold in their stomachs in order to squeeze into the elevator before the doors closed. The dining room was overcrowded, which was nothing new, so any attempt at conversation was a waste of breath. They joined the long line of other hungry staff members patiently waiting to be served. Carrying their lunch trays, they patiently searched for a vacant table. They eventually found one almost at the back of the cafeteria in a small alcove.

"This will do just fine," said Nancy. "I hope this food is as good as I hear it is." She looked around the room.

"The entire hospital seems to be here." Karen laughed. "I hear this new chef has added some heart-healthy meals to the menu, so I guess everyone's here to try them out."

"I hope it's not just healthy but tasty as well," Nancy replied, smiling.

They attacked their meals with gusto. "Mm, this chicken tastes heavenly," said Karen, licking her fingers.

"So does this chili. I wish I had the recipe. Not that it would come out tasting as nice as this anyway," replied Nancy. They both laughed and continued eating. Halfway through the meal, Nancy looked up.

"So, Karen, what did you want to talk about?" asked Nancy.

Karen carefully swallowed her mouthful of chicken before replying. "Do you remember when I came into the therapy room yesterday?"

"Yes, I remember. I was just finishing up a session with Luke," replied Nancy. "At the time I thought I was interrupting your session," continued Karen. "Later I came looking for you to apologize but got sidetracked and then completely forgot. Was that when Luke scared you?"

Nancy stopped eating before replying. "Yes, that was the time. I was so scared. When you came in, I was never so happy to see anyone in my life. That's why I left in such a hurry."

Karen looked at her. "I'm so very sorry. I should have been more observant." She reached over and squeezed Nancy's hand.

"It's not your fault," Nancy replied. "We were all taken in by his gorgeous smile, and all the while he was just a wolf in sheep's clothing."

"Well, we were all fooled, and it's not over yet," said Nancy as she looked around. "Remember Dr. Stone's warning. He wants us to be on guard. I still feel scared."

"So do I," replied Karen.

They finished lunch and wholeheartedly agreed that the food was very tasty and everything they expected and more. They made their way back to the department, each lost in her own thought about what might happen should Luke Foster decide to pay another visit.

26

For days after the meeting, the entire staff of the therapy department lived on pins and needles. Thankfully, Luke did not show his face at the center. Ms. Adams finally placed a call to the apartment but was told by the manager that he had moved out.

"Did he leave a forwarding address, Mr. Saunders?" asked Ms. Adams.

"No," he replied. "He told me he had no reason to leave a forwarding address as he wanted to forget that this place ever existed. He said that he had friends that would get him what he wanted, and he did not have to depend on anyone's handout. To tell the truth, I was not too unhappy to see him go."

"How did you find him as a tenant, Mr. Saunders?" she asked.

"What do you mean?" asked Mr. Saunders.

"I mean, did you find him to be a nice person? Did he get along with the other tenants? Things like that," asked Ms. Adams.

Mr. Saunders paused a moment. "You know," he said, deep in thought. "He was an interesting young man. One minute he was as sweet as pie, and the next minute, if you looked at him the wrong way, he would be ready to tear you apart. Those eyes…he had such expressive eyes. Even when he did not speak, his eyes said it all."

"I know what you mean. Did he get into a fight with anyone?" asked Ms. Adams. Mr. Saunders thought for a moment. "Well, I told him, as I do with all my tenants when they first move in, I do not tolerate any disruption from any of them. But I had to intervene a few times. Boy, did that young man have a temper? It looked like something was eating away at him from the inside."

"Did he ever say what it was? What was causing his anger," asked Ms. Adams.

"No, he never did," Mr. Saunders replied thoughtfully.

"Did he ever talk about his wife?" continued Ms. Adams.

"I didn't know he had a wife," said Mr. Saunders with surprise. "However, I did overhear him on his phone one day asking one of his no-good friends about how to go about finding a missing person."

"What did his friend say?" Ms. Adams asked.

"I think he told him to try the Internet or hire a private investigator. Luke got so angry when he heard about hiring a PI. He shouted nothing but obscenities asking where was he going to find money to hire a PI. I don't know what finally happened," said Mr. Saunders.

"Thank you, Mr. Saunders. I'll talk to you again soon," Ms. Adams replied.

27

As suspected, Luke's memory had completely returned for quite some time even though he had tried his best to keep this fact hidden. He was very annoyed that he had been caught red-handed lying to Ms. Adams. He was seeing red when he left the rehab center for the last time.

"I feel like going back there and teaching them all a lesson," he told his friend Carlos as they headed for their favorite watering hole.

Carlos was always cool and calmer than Luke, and so he was able to persuade him that now was not the time. He had no intention of aiding Luke with wreaking vengeance on anyone, but for the time being, he pretended to go along with him. "No, you don't want to do that. Wait until everything has calmed down, when they think you have forgotten, then that's the time you show them that you haven't," he told Luke.

"You're right," Luke replied. "I have to do better at keeping my feelings under control. Thanks, Carlos. You're always the voice of reason." He hugged Carlos hard. "You're a good friend, Carlos."

For now, Luke had had enough of small town New Hope and was itching to get moving. He had no idea where to go, but one thing he knew for sure; he did not want to return to Plains. He had had enough of those snooty rich people, and as far as he was concerned, his parents might as well be dead. He had not yet found a job, and the rehab center had informed him in writing that they were no longer responsible for his activities of daily living.

"I have no money, no job," he said angrily. "How am I supposed to live?" The fact was he was down to his last few dollars, and deep down he was really worried about his survival. Luckily, Carlos had told him he could stay with him until he made other plans. He was very thankful for the offer and was anxious to get moving. In addition, Mr. Saunders, the manager, had accosted him in the hallway earlier in the week.

"Luke, I was just on my way to see you. I received a letter from the rehab center informing me that they are no longer responsible for paying your rent."

"Yes, I know," he had replied and kept walking.

"Do you have a date in mind when you will be moving out?" asked Mr. Saunders.

"As soon as I know, I'll let you know," he had replied. The truth was that at the time he had no idea when or where he would live. Luckily, the situation was now resolved, and at least he now had a place to stay. A few days after talking to Mr. Saunders, his friend Carlos had come to his rescue and had offered him temporary shelter.

He didn't know how he was going to survive, but he would try to find some cash and then he would ditch this town. He had spent two months at the apartment, and as he packed his belongings, he realized how much he had accumulated during his short stay.

"At least I have some things I can call my own," he said, finishing the last of his packing. An hour later, Carlos came by to pick him up, and soon he was on his way out the door. As he reached the first floor, he bumped into Mr. Saunders.

"Luke," he said, surprised to see him leaving. "I didn't know you were leaving today?"

Luke gave him a look that would cause the normal man to tremble. But as Mr. Saunders, who had seen a great many things in his lifetime, often said, "It takes a much bigger man than you to cause me to tremble," he was unaffected.

"You wanted me gone, so I'm going, old man." Luke sneered.

As he headed out the door with Carlos, Mr. Saunders called after him. "Do you want to leave a forwarding address in case you get any mail?"

"Why would I want to do that?" Luke asked. "Anyone who needs to find me already knows how to find me," he said. With that, he headed out the door and into Carlos's broken-down van.

"Have a good life," said Mr. Saunders as the door closed behind him.

Carlos's place was nothing compared to the apartment he had just left, but Luke told himself that this was only going to be temporary, so he would try and make the best of it.

"As you know, I only have one bedroom, so you're going to have to sleep on the couch," Carlos informed him.

Realizing that beggars can't be choosers, Luke quickly replied, "Not a problem, man. I won't be here that long, so don't worry."

Luke settled in as best he could, and because he had no other options, he started looking for a job. However, finding a job proved to be more difficult than he anticipated, and unfortunately this did nothing to improve his disposition.

"This economy sucks," he complained to Carlos after coming back from yet another fruitless day of job hunting. "I've been pounding the pavement for the past week, and I have nothing to show for it."

"I know. I've been looking for a better job myself, but there's nothing out there, so I'm stuck myself. I wish I had one decent-paying job, then I would have the evenings off to do what I please," Carlos replied.

"What exactly is your job again?" asked Luke.

"I work at this garage in the mornings, then I wash dishes at a restaurant in the evenings," replied Carlos. "I could try and get you into the garage if you'd like."

"How are the tips?" asked Luke.

"Well, I don't really get tipped by the customers, but the waiters usually give me a few bucks. So with that plus minimum wage, plus the garage, I make out okay," replied Carlos with a shrug.

Luke thought for a while and then asked, "What do you do at the garage?"

"I clean up the garage, run errands, and do some odd jobs. I'm a gopher, for lack of a better word. Are you interested? If you are, I could talk to the boss, he's a really nice guy," said Carlos.

"Let me think about it, and I'll let you know in a few days," replied Luke.

So over the next few days, Luke doubled his effort trying to find a job, but again he found nothing. He really did not want to take a job working in a garage. He just did not feel like doing any dirty work; but the way things were looking, it seemed he might have no other choice.

Returning from another fruitless day of job hunting, he was physically and mentally exhausted. He sat on the couch with his hands between his knees, a bottle of beer in his hand, his shoulders hunched, and his head bowed. He looked and felt like a broken man. Things had not turned out exactly as he had anticipated, but he was not quite ready to give up.

"Carlos, did you ask your boss at the garage about a job for me?" he asked Carlos when he returned home.

"Yes. As a matter of fact, I was talking to him this morning. He said if you were interested, you should come in to talk with him on Monday," Carlos replied.

"Okay, I'll do that. I've tried everything else, but there're just no jobs out there for me. If I had a college degree, then it would be different, so I'm willing to give it a try." He sighed deeply at the thought of what he must do. "I guess I can't keep taking your kindness for granted, Carlos."

"Don't feel that way. You'll be fine. I just know it," Carlos replied.

28

They hit the clubs over the weekend and partied like they didn't have a care. It was difficult, but Luke tried hard to control his alcohol intake. He had been trying for quite some time now, and it was proving to be more difficult than he had anticipated. He had fallen off the wagon a few times, but he still wasn't ready to give up on himself just yet. He had overindulged on more than one occasion, and Carlos remembered having quite a difficult time getting him back to the apartment. At that time, he had seen a side of Luke that he hoped he never had to see again.

"Man, you are one mean drunk," Carlos had told him when he had sobered up.

"What did I do?" Luke had asked worriedly.

"Look at my eyes. I can hardly see out of the right one. You almost blinded me. If you decide to drink that much again, you're on your own. I will not place my life in danger again trying to get you home," said Carlos angrily.

"I'm so sorry, Carlos. It won't happen again, I promise," Luke had replied. So although he would have Sunday to sleep it off, Luke made sure he reigned in his desire to overindulge. After all, he did not want to blow his chances of getting the job at the garage.

When Monday morning rolled around, Luke presented himself at Mike's garage at nine o'clock. He doubted that Mike would want him to start working right away, but just in case, he was dressed respectably and ready for the task. If that's what it took to convince Mike he desperately needed the job, then that's what he would do.

As he entered the garage, he was bombarded by the pervasive smell of motor oil, tires, lubricating fluid, and the continuous noise from pneumonic drills. Pieces of car parts were scattered around the garage floor, making it unsafe for anyone who did not work there. Mechanics in their greasy overalls bustled around, replacing parts to the various cars. He hesitated for a moment and watched. He recalled the days when he worked in a place similar to this. He sighed deeply. *Boy, how I used to enjoy getting my hands dirty. For some reason, I've lost that desire.*

He walked out and looked around, trying to locate the office. Unable to find it, he returned to the work area and approached one of the mechanics. His face and overalls were so greasy Luke could barely make out his facial features. Tearing his eyes away from the man's greasy face, he asked, "I'm here to see Mike. Is he around?"

The man looked at him and shouted, "I can't hear you! You'll have to speak up if you want me to hear you!"

Luke had no choice, so he raised his voice. "I'm here to see Mike. Can you tell me where he is?"

"He's probably in the office!" the mechanic shouted back, pointing to the right.

"Thank you!" Luke shouted back and headed in the direction to which the man pointed.

He soon came to a room with a sign that said "Office" hanging askew on the door. On entering, he saw that it was nothing more than a small room with a few old chairs scattered around and a three-legged coffee table leaning against one wall. The walls were dirty and greasy, making it impossible to tell what the original color once was. Staring at it, Luke couldn't help himself. *I wonder when this wall received a coat of paint.*

He continued taking in his surroundings. In one corner, a pot stood with some dried leaves on something that resembled a stalk. It could have been a plant at some point, but that must have been a very long time ago. Looking at the floor, it was hard to tell the last time it was swept. Finally, the man sitting behind the overcrowded table looked up from the papers he was busy sorting. A large cigar dangled from the corner of his mouth, and his overall looked as if it had seen better days. His face was bloated and discolored, and his hair was a disheveled curly mix of grey and black—more grey than black. He heaved his bulk up from the chair and moved toward Luke, his greasy right hand outstretched.

Hi, I'm Mike. You must be Luke."

Luke hesitated but only for a moment. Not wanting to seem inhospitable to the man who might be his future boss, he shook the man's hands enthusiastically. He was rewarded with a rough, greasy feel to his hands, which he tried his best to ignore. "Yes, sir, I'm Luke. Carlos said I should come in and see you about a job?"

"Yes, yes. Sorry I can't offer you a seat," said Mike, looking around at the chaos. "But we can talk right here, if you don't mind." As he talked, he walked back to the table that was serving as a desk.

"Tell me," he asked Luke. "Do you know anything about computers? I have this machine, but no one knows how to use it. I had someone here from the agency a few weeks ago, but she only stayed two days. What I need is someone who can clean up and organize the office so I can find things when I need them."

As he talked, he coughed a long, hacking cough that turned his face a dusky red. Luke discreetly moved back to avoid being sprayed with tobacco juice. *Talk about a smoker's cough,* Luke thought to himself. *I'm so glad I never got hooked on cigarettes.*

"Yes, sir. I can use a computer," replied Luke. Taking another look around at the clutter, Luke continued. "Looks like a lot of work, but I can certainly try. When would you like me to start?" he asked.

"Can you start today?" Mike asked.

"Yes, sir," replied Luke, almost smiling. *Good thing I came in ready for work*, he thought.

A look of relief came over Mike's face. "You're a lifesaver, Luke. Now, about your pay, how much do you expect?"

He was not familiar with the hourly rates for this type of job, but Luke was determined not to be shortchanged. The wheels in his head started turning. Looking Mike in the eyes, he asked, "How much were you paying the girl from the agency?"

"The regular going rate of seven dollars an hour," said Mike.

"Let's make it ten dollars. I get weekends and holidays off, two weeks' vacation a year, and you've got yourself a deal." Luke smiled.

Mike looked at him and returned the smile. "You drive a hard bargain, Luke. I guess I've met my match. Let's make that eight, and we'll talk some more about your days off, but for now, you're hired." He again held out his hand, and Luke had no choice but to shake it. Before hurrying out to the garage, Mike turned to Luke. "Ms. Gibson will be picking up her car this evening. Take care of the paperwork, will you? It's sitting on the table somewhere."

"No problem," Luke replied. Taking another long look around the office, Luke sighed as he started sorting through the jumble of paper on what passed for a desk.

"The first on my list of things to do is to order a real desk," he said. "I'll be in charge of handling all that money, imagine that!" He smiled to himself as he went about sorting out the mess. By the time lunchtime rolled around, he had barely made a dent in the pile of papers. He decided he needed to talk to Mike about spending some money toward bringing the office into the twenty-first century.

He opened the door leading into the garage. His eardrums were immediately bombarded by the noise. *I hope I can get used to this noise*, he thought to himself. He called out to Mike, but his voice was lost amid the chaos of the garage. Mike was headed toward one of the tow trucks, so Luke intercepted him before he drove off.

"Mike, can I talk to you for a minute?" he called out.

Mike looked at him impatiently, his hand on the keys ready to start the engine. "Can this wait until I get back? I'm going to pick up lunch," he replied. "Oh, by the way, we call in every day to the diner down the street and order lunch. Someone then has to pick it up, they don't deliver. I forgot you were here. Do you want me to bring you back something?" he asked.

"Yes. I'd love a pastrami on whole wheat with a large wedge of pickle, also a large coke. I hope you don't mind."

"No, not at all," Mike replied. "By the way, starting tomorrow, ordering and picking up lunch will be part of your job." He started the truck and drove off without waiting for a reply.

Luke groaned. "Well, thank you very much," he said to himself. Heading back to the office, he decided this was as good a time as any to introduce himself to the other workers, as it was obvious that Mike was not about to do so. He made an about face and headed toward the work area. There was a lull in the usual bedlam, so he decided to seize the moment.

"Hey, guys," he called out. "I don't know if Mike told you, but I'm Luke. I'm going to be working in the office. I'm a friend of Carlos's."

Faces looked up from under car hoods, bodies rolled out from under cars, and visors were raised as they all looked at Luke. As if previously rehearsed, they all called out in unison, "Hey, Luke. Good to see you, man. Welcome to bedlam."

"Make sure my paycheck is correct this week," shouted a big grizzly looking mechanic in the process of doing an oil change. Everyone laughed.

"I'll see what I can do," Luke replied, laughing. He hung around for a while, talking to the men until the sound of Mike's truck broke into their conversation.

"I hope he got my order right today. I'm tired of not getting what I ordered," moaned one mechanic, sliding out from under a car close by. Mike pulled into the garage and barely had time to park before he was surrounded. He began calling out names as he dug into the box overflowing with lunch orders.

"Dave, Sam, Buzz, Rick…Don't blame me if you get the wrong order," he said. "Talk to Carla at the diner if you have a problem. She took the orders."

They all seemed to have received the correct orders because soon they were all sitting down on any available box, tire, or bench they could find. For a while, all that was heard was the sound of lips smacking, sodas guzzling, and loud burping.

29

By the end of the first week, Luke had managed to convince Mike to buy a new desk, a chair, and a file cabinet for the office.

"I don't know why you need all these things?" Mike complained daily.

"Because in order to keep things in any semblance of order, you need to be organized. I can't keep putting things in cardboard boxes or leaving them on the table. You need to have a system in place," Luke kept telling him. However, Mike always seemed to conveniently forget.

Within a few weeks, the dirty, disorganized space that Luke had inherited started looking like a real office. The walls had received a much-needed coat of paint, and there were now nice clean chairs, a coffee table, and a rack with magazines and newspapers that were delivered daily. There was still a lot to be done, but at least it was a start. He was now able to find what he needed without wasting too much time searching. He knew that in order to get things looking even better, he would have to ask Mike to spend more money.

"He's not going to like that, and I'm certainly not looking forward to asking him," Luke told himself. "But it has to be done."

He was not well versed on using the computer, but each day he learned a bit more. And so he created an organized system that could keep detailed records on each customer transaction. He had managed to talk Mike into purchasing accounting software and some filing cabinets to keep things more organized. He also put in place a system for billing, a functional accounts receivable bookkeeping system, and an accounts payable system.

Much to his surprise, he realized he was really enjoying his job. In his spare time, he surfed the Internet looking for sites devoted to finding lost friends, relatives, or loved ones. His memory regarding Margaret had completely returned, and his most urgent need was to find her. He had no idea where she had gone. In fact, he had no idea if she was alive, dead, or in which state she now lived. Deep down he knew one thing was sure—he had no intention of giving up his search. The more he thought about her, the more he doubled his efforts to find her.

The biggest stumbling block was that with every thought of her, his anger would boil. A sudden pressure would start building in the back of his head, travel through his neck, and spread upward through his entire head. The feeling was so intense he felt as if his head would explode. "Maybe I have a brain tumor," he once told himself. Nothing he tried would bring him relief. If he was at work, he would head for the men's room and lock himself in one of the stalls until the pain subsided. He had no control over his rage toward her. It was so overwhelming; at times he thought that he must be going mad.

He did his best not to think too much about her while at work, but this was impossible as he had no home computer. He could not afford to buy one for himself, so he had no choice but to use the one at work. He liked his job and wanted to hold on to it for as long as possible, and doing anything to jeopardize it was the last thing he wanted. He and Mike got on well, but still Mike was the boss, and after all, this was a place of business.

It was now six months since Luke had started working at the garage, and he was still sleeping on Carlos's couch. He had managed to squirrel away some money from his paychecks as he planned to find an apartment of his own very soon. He was extremely thankful for Carlos's generosity, but the lack of privacy grated on his nerve. He had no place to entertain friends; after all, he was a handsome young man with needs.

Summer had arrived, and he was desperate to get his own place. The past weekend he had gone looking at a few places, but so far, what he had seen was not worth the price they were asking. These apartments were all located in Carlos's neighborhood, but he wanted to check other neighborhoods close by to see how they compared.

For the upcoming weekend, he had made an appointment to visit an apartment not far from where he was currently staying. He had seen the advertisement in one of the local papers and had called out of curiosity. The realtor had sounded quite friendly when he called, so he was quite anxious to take a look.

"These apartments were recently renovated and are in excellent condition. The rent is also very reasonable. Why don't you come by and take a look? Then you can make a decision," Ron the realtor had told him. Not wanting to miss out on a good deal, Luke made an appointment and was looking forward to the weekend. He asked Carlos to accompany him so he could at least get a second opinion.

30

Luke spent a restless night, his mind refusing to shut down. All he could think about were the new apartments that Ron was going to show him. Sunday morning rolled around bright and sunny, and as tired as he was, he was still anxious to get going. He had a small breakfast of coffee and a bagel then headed out, dragging Carlos along.

"Luke, this is Sunday. It's the only morning that I get to sleep late. Why do you have to go this early?" Carlos moaned.

"I want to be sure that all the good apartments aren't taken, in case I decide to get one. Don't you want me off your couch?" Luke replied as they hurried to the bus station. They passed by graffiti-covered buildings with overflowing garbage cans and broken bottles littering the sidewalks. As they skirted the potential danger of injury from broken glass, Luke thought to himself, *I really need to get out of this neighborhood.* Although it was only nine o'clock in the morning, kids still dressed in clothes they had worn to bed the night before were already sitting on the steps, talking loudly and yelling at each other.

"Hold up, Luke. I can't walk as fast as you. I'm used to driving," moaned Carlos, struggling to keep up with Luke.

"Walking is good for you, Carlos. Maybe it's a good reason your car is in the shop. This gives you a chance to get in some well-needed exercise." He laughed and breathed deeply, feeling rejuvenated.

Carlos hurried along as best he could. It was Sunday, and the buses were running far and few in between. Reaching the bus stop, they were just in time to see the taillight of one bus that had just gone by. This meant they had quite a long wait before the next one arrived. This gave Carlos enough time to sit and catch his breath while Luke paced like a caged tiger raring to go.

Finally, the bus arrived, and they gladly escaped the summer heat into the bus' cool interior. It was half-empty, so they had their choice of seats. In half an hour, they arrived at the realtor's office. After the introductions were made, the realtor drove them to the apartment building, which was only a few minutes from the office.

"This is a very nice neighborhood," said Carlos as they drove up and parked outside the building. "I didn't know there were such nice areas in New Hope."

"Yes," replied Ron. "This area is undergoing a resurgence. This is the first building to be renovated. Soon you won't be able to recognize this neighborhood. This building used to be an old warehouse, but it was recently bought by some rich developers and converted into these beautiful apartments."

The building was painted in a shade of soft yellow with the window trims in a cool shade of green. Tall oak trees lining the sides and back of the building provided just the right amount of privacy and shading without blocking the natural view. Flowering plants gave off a pleasant aroma that filled the air and contributed to the creation of a magnificent landscape.

"Luke, do you like what you've seen so far?" asked Ron.

"Yes, I do. I like everything so far. If the inside is as nice as the outside, then you could say you have a deal," Luke replied, smiling.

"But you haven't even heard the price as yet," Ron replied. Luke was too busy enjoying the landscape to reply.

Ron opened the front door and waited for Luke and Carlos to enter. They stepped into a foyer decorated with large pots of green shrubs and beautiful artwork covering the walls. Looking around, they were speechless as they took in their surroundings.

"We are definitely not in Kansas anymore," said Luke, smiling at Carlos while staring from one end of the foyer to the next. Ron led them toward the elevator. "Let's go up to the sixth floor so you can enjoy the view. Luke, I know you said you wanted a one-bedroom, but those go very fast, and right now there's none left, so I'm going to show you a two-bedroom."

Luke paled. "Hold on, Ron. I don't know if I'll be able to afford a two-bedroom. My finances are…ah…somewhat limited," he stammered.

"Don't worry, the price is not that much different, and if you really like it, I can try and work out a deal," said Ron.

The elevator ride was so fast and smooth they weren't even sure they were moving until a soft ding announced their arrival on the sixth floor.

"Man, that was one smooth ride," said Carlos as the doors softly slid open. Ron took them a short way down the corridor and opened the door to the two-bedroom apartment.

Luke was blown away!

They entered a hallway that led directly into the living room. To the right was a dining room capable of seating a party of ten. Looking around the room, Luke could not believe his eyes.

"Luke, this is an open floor plan," said Ron. "Each room opens out into the other. With this design, entertaining is so much more enjoyable. You'll be able to see all your guests, and no one will feel excluded. This is the latest design in housing," he continued as he headed for the kitchen.

"This is your kitchen. The appliances are all modern and high-end." Luke was speechless. These were the most beautiful appliances he had seen since he started searching for an apartment. "And here's the balcony," Ron continued.

They followed Ron toward the door leading from the living room onto the balcony, which ran the entire length of the apartment. There was nothing to block the view or the natural light. The trees were tall and well spaced and located a good distance from the building. Looking over the treetops, the view of the city's skyline in the distance was unstoppable.

Closing his eyes, his head thrown back, Luke took a deep breath. "This is living," he murmured. "Oh! This is going to be nonstop partying."

"I can see that you like it," said Ron, smiling.

"No, Ron, I don't like it," Luke replied. "I love it!"

"Would you like to see the bedrooms?" asked Ron. "They're just as nice."

Mesmerized, Luke and Carlos followed Ron into the bedrooms. "I love these closets, they're so spacious. I'll need to buy a lot more clothes," said Luke.

As they continued looking around, Ron's cell phone rang. He retrieved it and checked the number before excusing himself to take the call. Finishing the call, he returned inside. "Excuse me, Luke. This must be your lucky day. Remember I told you that single bedrooms are hard to come by? That was my office calling to say that the buyer of the only single bedroom on this floor just called the office. Unfortunately for them and fortunately for you, they had some family problems and can no longer go through with the deal. Would you like to see it? It's just down the hall."

"Okay, but I think I've already seen what I want," Luke replied.

They followed Ron down the hallway to look at the single bedroom. It was nice and cozy with all the amenities of the first apartment, just on a smaller scale. It even contained an en suite, which was a bit small but very modern and well designed.

"Well, what do you think?" asked Ron.

"Very nice, but I know what I like, and I've already seen it," replied Luke.

Ron hesitated. "Correct me if I'm wrong, but I thought you wanted a one-bedroom?"

"Well, I've changed my mind," replied Luke smugly.

"Okay, as long as you're sure. Let me lock up, and then we can head back to the office and talk price," said Ron.

It was a quiet ride back to Ron's office. Luke couldn't help but daydream about enjoying life in his spacious two-bedroom apartment. Ron had not quoted a price, but Luke knew that this apartment would not be cheap, but after all, it was only money.

"Carlos," Luke asked. "You're so quiet. Did you like the place?"

"Yes, I love it," replied Carlos. "But it looks so expensive. I don't think you'll be able to afford it."

"I don't know either, but I'm waiting for Ron to work his magic so I'll be able to afford it," he replied, laughing. Soon they were all relaxing in Ron's office, waiting for Ron to give them the good news. When Ron thought that Luke was relaxed and ready, he moved in for the kill.

"So, Luke, how much do you think that beautiful apartment that you love so much will cost you monthly?"

Luke sat up straight in his chair and looked at Ron. "Because this is a new building that's renting for the first time, I'm going to take a wild guess and say about twelve hundred dollars a month," he said.

Ron laughed as he adjusted his glasses. "When was the last time you rented an apartment, Luke? Those prices haven't been around for the past five years."

Luke straightened in his chair, feeling a bit foolish. "That's too low? So how much does it cost?"

Ron cleared his throat. "Are you ready for this?" he asked.

"Yes, I am," replied Luke hesitantly.

"Well," said Ron. "The monthly rent is two thousand five hundred dollars. Before you can move into this apartment, you will need to deposit one month's rent plus one month's security."

Luke quickly did the math. "You mean I'll need five thousand dollars up front before I can move in?" he asked, surprised.

Ron nodded. "Yes, you do."

"But you said you could work your magic…w-what happened?" stuttered Luke.

"This is my magic at work," Ron replied, laughing. "I was able to significantly reduce the asking price as promised in order to let you have it."

"I can't imagine how much it cost before you worked your magic," Luke replied, looking at Ron.

"You don't want to know." Ron shook his head and kept on smiling.

Luke could see his dreams crumbling before his eyes. Never one to be easily deterred, he thought to himself, *I'll find a way to get around this temporary obstacle.*

Realizing no answer was forthcoming, Ron finally broke the silence. "I told you to consider the one-bedroom apartment," said Ron. Luke gave no answer. He almost forgot that Carlos was there until he heard his voice.

"Luke, I think you should take the one-bedroom. It has to be less expensive, and you really don't need all that space."

Luke did not reply. "Just out of curiosity, how much will the one-bedroom cost?" Luke asked.

Ron shuffled through the papers on his desk. "Here we are. The one-bedroom is fifteen hundred a month. That's pretty affordable, wouldn't you say?"

"Ron, can I have some time to think this through?" asked Luke.

"How much time are we talking about?" Ron asked.

"Just a few days," replied Luke. "I need to think about this some more."

"Exactly which apartment are you considering?" asked Ron.

"Well, you know I'd love to have the two bedrooms, but I'll let you know."

"Okay," replied Ron, taking a deep breath. "Don't forget what I said. This won't be around for long, so if I don't hear from you by Wednesday…"

"You'll hear from me. I promise," Luke replied, rising to go.

Ron stood up and extended his hands to Luke. "Okay, Luke. It's all up to you."

Luke and Carlos left the real estate office and made their way back to their apartment with Luke deep in thought.

31

The wheels continued turning so fast in Luke's head; he was having a hard time keeping up with his thoughts. He spent a restless night, and by the time daylight rolled around, he had made a decision.

Luke left the apartment early without seeing Carlos or even having his usual morning coffee. He was the first to arrive at the garage. He double-checked to make sure there was no one present in the garage. Satisfied, he headed for the office, but today he had more than work on his mind. He made sure the office door was locked and the lights off. New plantation blinds had been installed at the windows, so he made sure they were completely closed. As luck would have it, he had been running late on Friday and was unable to make the usual bank deposit. He had locked the money in the file cabinet, and this was going to come in extremely handy today.

"If Mike knew that I did this, he would kill me," he said to himself. He headed to the file cabinet and opened the bottom drawer. Moving the files toward the front, he could see the manila envelope just where he had left it. As he reached in to retrieve it, he heard a sound that made him hesitate.

"Mike," he called out nervously. "Is that you?" He received no reply.

He listened intensely, but the sound was not repeated, so he picked up the envelope and hurriedly placed it in his desk drawer. His heart was pounding so hard he was having difficulty breathing. After listening for a while, he withdrew the envelope again, removed half of the larger bills and placed them in another envelope, then placed the rest in the bank's night deposit bag.

By then the garage had started coming to life, and no sooner had he placed the bag out of sight than Mike entered the office. His trademark cigar dangled from the corner of his mouth as usual. He was surprised to find Luke in the office.

"Hi, Luke. You're early today. Why is the door locked?" he asked.

"Hi, Mike," Luke replied. "I had some stuff I needed to take care of, so I decided to come in a bit early."

"Why are the lights off?" asked Mike, looking around. "This place is like a tomb," he continued as he started opening the blinds and turning on the lights. "I was trying to save you a few dollars on the electricity. The AC burns enough as it is," replied Luke, smiling nervously.

"Don't worry about that. I don't want you going blind for a few dollars." Mike deposited a bunch of papers on the desk and headed toward the garage, Luke's eyes watching his every move. Suddenly he turned, hands on the door handle. "Did you make that deposit on Friday like I asked?"

"Of course, I did. You know you can depend on me, Mike." He laughed nervously.

Mike gave him a long look. "Are you okay, Luke?"

"Yes, I'm fine," he replied. "Why do you ask?"

"Oh," he shrugged. "You just seem a bit jumpy."

"Oh, I had a busy weekend. Didn't get enough sleep, but I'll be fine," he replied, trying to appear nonchalant. He gave Luke another long look of concern then headed to the garage work area. Luke took a deep breath. "That was too close for comfort," he said to himself. He couldn't wait for lunchtime so he could head to the bank and make the deposit.

"I hope he won't get a chance to check the books anytime soon. If he does, I'm in big trouble. It's just a loan. I'll pay him back soon," he told himself.

Things got busy at the garage with customers dropping off and picking up their cars, so Luke never got a chance to visit the bank. Matter of fact, he had to work through lunch, so this gave him an excuse to leave work a bit earlier than usual. He headed for the bank and made the deposit before going home. Reaching the apartment, he remembered that Carlos was working late, but he was desperate to talk to someone. He began nervously pacing the floor.

Finally, Carlos arrived home. The moment Luke heard the key in the lock, he rushed over and yanked the door open. Carlos almost lost his footing as the door was wrenched from his hand. He was about to let Luke have it, but one look at his face and he swallowed his words.

"Hey, what's wrong with you? You look terrible," said Carlos.

"Never mind about that. Guess what?" Not waiting for a reply, Luke blurted out. "I have the money."

"What money?" asked Carlos, staring blankly at Luke.

"The down payment on the apartment," replied Luke.

Carlos's face lit up as he moved to hug Luke. "Oh, Mike gave you a loan? That's so nice. That Mike is such a nice guy. I'm happy for you, man."

"No, you don't understand," Luke said, anxiety making his voice harsh. He started pacing the floor again.

Carlos shook his head, puzzled. "Understand what? Luke, you should be happy. Now you can call Ron and tell him you have the money."

Unable to look Carlos in the eye, Luke stuttered, "M-Mike did not loan me the money. I stole…I mean I borrowed it. I'll pay him back."

"You did what?" Carlos exploded. "I helped you get that job, and now you're stealing from Mike? I recommended you for that job. I really don't know you, do I, Luke?"

"I said I'll pay him back!" Luke shouted angrily.

"How and when?" asked Carlos.

"Don't worry. I'll find a way. Furthermore, this is none of your business."

"You made it my business when you told me about it!" shouted Carlos angrily. "I think you'd better find another place to stay, Luke. I can't afford to harbor a thief in my apartment." He walked out of the room, looking at Luke with disgust.

"Okay, if that's what you want. I'll leave in the morning!" Luke shouted. He started angrily throwing his clothes and other belongings into a pillowcase in readiness for his departure in the morning.

32

When morning arrived, he began lugging his personal stuff to his car in readiness to begin his new life. For a minute, he felt bad that he was leaving without saying good-bye to Carlos, but the thought of his new apartment and the new life that lay ahead soon drove it from his mind. Arriving at work, he booted up the computer, but instead of logging on to the garage's website, he did an Internet search. He typed in "find an old friend" and restlessly waited to see what would happen. A site popped up asking him to type the person's name, age, and the last known address. He entered all the required information then waited. He was then asked to create an account and add his credit card information. He had no intention of giving out his private information, so he logged off and started on the day's work. However, he could not focus on his work, and kept making stupid mistakes. He decided to revisit the Internet, but instead of looking for a lost friend, he decided to google a private investigator. He was rewarded with a number of choices, so he decided to take a chance and call the first investigator listed. Halfway through dialing, he changed his mind and decided to call Ron instead.

After the confrontation with Carlos last night, he had decided that he had had enough of sleeping on Carlos's couch. So first thing this morning, he had packed his belongings and tossed them in the back of the old car that Mike had sold him not long after he had started working there. He quickly dialed Ron's number before losing his nerve. Ron picked up after the second ring.

"Hey, Ron, this is Luke Foster."

"Hi, Luke. It's so nice hearing from you. Does this mean you've made your decision?"

"Yes, I have," replied Luke. "When can I come over?"

"How about this evening around five? Is that a good time for you?" asked Ron.

"That will be fine. I'll see you then." Luke hung up, his heart hammering in his chest.

After taking Mike's money, he had been undecided about going through with renting the apartment. At one point, he even thought about returning it, but then Carlos had to interfere. That made him so mad that he decided there and then to follow through with his plan.

He was on tenterhooks all day, so as soon as the clock struck four, he left the office and headed out for his meeting with Ron. All the way to the realtor's office, he kept picturing how he would decorate his new apartment.

"I don't have a lot of money for expensive furniture right now, so I guess I'll have to live the Spartan lifestyle for a while," he said to himself. Luke soon arrived at the office, and Ron welcomed him like a long lost friend while thinking how he was going to spend his commission.

"Luke," he said, smiling and slapping him on the back. "I'm glad to see you. Come on in. Have a seat, please." Before he sat down, Ron asked, "Would you like a drink?"

"No, thanks," Luke replied.

"Okay then, let's get down to business. So which apartment have you decided on?" asked Ron.

"I think I'm going with the two-bedroom," said Luke.

"Are you sure?" asked Ron. Luke nodded yes. A big smile came over Ron's face. "Good decision, Luke. You will not be sorry. Would you like to take another look at it before signing the lease?"

"No. I'm sure," Luke replied.

Ron brought out what seemed like a million pieces of papers. He briefly explained the purpose of each, then he had Luke affix his signature.

"Seems like a lot of papers to sign," Luke said tentatively.

"Well, this is a big step for you. We want to be sure that everything is up front and legal. Make sure you read through the lease agreement thoroughly. I will give you copies of each. Do you have any questions for me before I give you the keys?" asked Ron.

"Not that I can think of," replied Luke. And so the die was cast, and there was no turning back. Luke was now the tenant of a brand new two-bedroom apartment at two thousand five hundred dollars a month for the next year.

"Okay," said Ron, handing him a set of keys. "If you have any questions about anything, please give me a call." They shook hands, and Luke left the office. A part of him felt ecstatic, but another part was deeply worried.

"I hope I made the right choice," he said to himself as he headed over to his new apartment. He was determined to enjoy himself, so he got in his car, turned the radio to maximum volume, and rocked to the sound of the music. As his foot hit the accelerator and the car picked up speed, he gave a loud whoop. "Party central!" he yelled. He could not recall ever feeling as happy as he did right now!

33

Margaret settled down and started her new life in Sycamore, Connecticut, as a waitress at the Blue Bird diner. Her past life was never far from her mind, and sometimes she wondered if she had dreamt it all. At first she had had frequent nightmares in which Luke was strangling her or pounding her with a baseball bat. She would wake up screaming, drenched in sweat, and gasping for air. Many were the nights that Carol had gone in just to hold her and calm her down.

"It's only a dream, Margaret," she would say, rocking her gently. "Don't worry, it's not real. You're safe here, go back to sleep." It would take a while before she eventually fell back to sleep, but it was never a sound sleep. She would wake up feeling and looking as tired as when she went to bed. Try as she might, she could not help but think back to that fateful night when she made her escape. She often wondered how her life would have turned out had she not fled.

"I'd probably be dead," she told herself.

Carol had been an angel sent to rescue her that night, and Margaret was always thankful to God for that. Physically she was far away from Luke Foster, but mentally he was right there with her. At times she was positive that she was being followed and would constantly look over her shoulder when walking by herself, so for a while she never went out alone.

She often wondered what happened to him after his car nose-dived off the Plains drawbridge. After arriving in Sycamore, she had anxiously searched the newspapers, listened to the news, and even searched the Internet for any article pertaining to the accident, but there had been no mention of it. She had asked Carol on more than one occasion, "Carol, do you think he's dead?" to which Carol would respond, "I don't know, but don't worry. Even if he's alive, how would he find you? You're far away from Plains. Try and forget about him." She would take Carol's advice and try to put the entire incident behind her, but ultimately the thought would return, and she would start worrying all over again.

"You have to stop making yourself crazy," Carol told her sympathetically.

"You don't know him," she replied anxiously. "He's mean and evil, and I'm sure if he finds me, he will kill me. No matter what I do, he's never far from my mind."

The happiest times for Margaret was when she was working and helping others. Work left her with very little time to worry, allowing her to focus on others and not be bogged down with the problems of her past life. However, at the end of her work day, her mind would return to Luke. This resulted in many sleepless nights. Carol could no longer stand to see her friend suffer any longer.

"You can't continue this way, Margaret. If you don't get some sleep, you'll die from exhaustion," she told her. "Why not come with me to see my doctor?"

"What will he do for me? Prescribe sleeping pills? I don't want to get hooked on sleeping pills," she responded sluggishly.

"Well, you can at least talk to him. Sometimes it helps just by talking to someone. Maybe he'll have some suggestions that will help," Carol told her.

Finally, after an accident with a customer's order at the diner, she relented and agreed that she needed help. And so she went and saw Carol's doctor. He was an older gentleman, very kind and patient, and an excellent listener. Although Margaret could not remember her father clearly, she thought of him as a father figure. She felt very relaxed in his presence and was able to tell him some of her concerns.

He listened attentively to Margaret and prescribed a mild sleeping pill. "This should help you relax so you can get some sleep. It's very mild and won't leave you feeling groggy in the morning. Let me know how this works, and call me if there's any problem," he told her before she left his office.

"Thank you, Dr. King," Margaret replied.

Dr. King was right, and she was finally able to sleep soundly through the night. The nightmares soon disappeared, and after a few weeks, she no longer needed the pills. Feeling rejuvenated, she continued to enjoy her job and now looked forward to going to work. She carefully saved her tips and a portion of her paycheck while contributing her portion toward her stay at Carol's apartment.

Of all the regular customers that frequented the diner, Margaret especially liked a cute older African American couple, Diane and Arthur Turnbull. They were in their mid-eighties, and from the stories they told, it was clear they had been through unspeakable experiences throughout their lives. Life had not always been easy for them, but it was difficult to tell from the way they behaved. They were always bubbly as they told the most outrageous stories. They always had the other customers in stitches. At times the diner almost seemed like a comic relief convention.

"Never let anyone tell you how to live your life," Diane often told Margaret. "It's your life, and you alone are responsible for your actions. Whether you fail or succeed, you have no one to blame but yourself." Margaret listened carefully to Diane and decided to take her advice to heart. She decided to live her life by a set of rules. First, she resolved to attend church regularly and then get a profession rather than just a job, and finally, she would move into her own apartment.

Soon she started going to church regularly and only stayed away when she had to work on Sundays. She started volunteering at the women's shelter, and soon she enrolled for evening courses at the community college. The more she kept busy, the less time she had to think about Luke, and the less fear she felt. As she began to take control of her life, things slowly started to change. She felt stronger, calmer, and more at peace with herself. Carol began to see the changes in her and asked, "You seem so much happier of late. What's your secret?"

"Well, I've decided not to let anyone control my life anymore, no one except God. So I've given him all my fears and worries. Now I feel lighter and happier, like a burden has been lifted from my shoulders." She smiled, and her face radiated all the joy she felt inside. Carol hugged her. "I'm so happy for you, my friend. It's so good to see you smile."

34

"Furnishing an apartment is not as easy as I thought," said Luke to himself as he stood looking at all the empty space. It was now two months since he had moved in, and so far, he had only managed to buy a bed and a few pots and pans. Paper plates and plastic flatware were his dishes of choice.

"Who needs to be washing dishes when I can just throw them in the garbage?" he asked himself. "I'm better off using that money to pay the rent."

As for replacing Mike's money, he refused to think too much about it. He consoled himself with the thought that "Mike does not need it right away, I do. So why worry?"

Almost every weekend, there was a party at his place. His motto to his friends was, "No one shows up with empty hands." With that mindset, he never had to spend too much of his own money to finance his parties. There was always more than enough alcohol to keep the party going, and he was always the life of the party, or so his friends told him. However, when he was alone, he worried about the choices he had made. Money was in short supply, and even though he was able to pay his monthly rent, the credit card bills were starting to pile up.

For the past two months, he was able to pay only the minimum on his credit cards, yet he had no choice but to continue using them. Each week he managed to skim a few dollars from the money Mike had entrusted to him. But even with that, it was still a struggle making ends meet while maintaining the charade.

I don't know how much longer I can keep doing this, he thought to himself. *I'll have to start putting it back before he finds out.*

It was now Sunday, and all his friends had left for home to sleep off the effects of Saturday night's party. Luke could not sleep. He had too much on his mind. He thought the alcohol would have drowned out his thoughts, but that was just not happening. Sitting on the balcony by himself, his thoughts drifted to Carlos. He started pacing as his mind kept racing. He had not talked to him since the day he had abruptly left his apartment.

"I should at least tell him thanks for letting me stay on his couch all that time," he said to himself. "In addition, he knows my secret. They say to keep your friends close but your enemies closer."

Putting thought into action, he picked up his cell phone and dialed Carlos. *I hope he'll talk to me, but I wouldn't blame him if he refuses to take my call,* Luke thought to himself. The phone rang and rang.

He was about to disconnect when Carlos answered. "What do you want Luke?" he asked angrily.

"Is that any way to talk to your old buddy?" Luke asked.

"Buddy?" laughed Carlos sarcastically. "No, Luke, you're not my buddy. I don't have thieves for buddies. By the way, have you replaced Mike's money?"

Luke did not reply.

"I didn't think so," said Carlos.

He couldn't think of an answer that would appease Carlos, so he decided to change the subject. "Listen, Carlos. I'm having some friends over on Friday night. I'd like you to come. After all, you haven't seen my new place since I moved in."

"Thanks for the invitation, Luke, but I'm going to be busy." He was about to hang up but decided to give Luke something to think about. "Oh, by the way, you have two weeks to replace Mike's money, or your little secret will be out. Bye, Luke."

"You can't do that to me—" Luke yelled angrily, but he was talking to a dead phone. Carlos had already hung up. Anger washed over Luke. He sprang from his chair and ran to the kitchen. With a loud yell, he rammed the phone down hard on top of the granite counter top with such force, it broke into several small pieces. He desperately needed an outlet to release this anger.

"I need a drink," he said. He hurriedly opened the liquor cabinet, but it was empty, so he grabbed his car keys and headed out the door. In no mood to wait for the elevator, he bounded down the stairs two at a time, slamming the door as he exited onto the parking lot.

He had every intention of confronting Carlos, so he jumped in his car, turned the key, but it refused to start. Looking at the dashboard, he realized that the gas gauge was pointing to empty. He remembered that he had planned to visit the gas station on Friday evening after work but had not left the apartment since. His head felt like it was about to explode.

From prior experience, he knew that release of his anger was imperative to ease the pressure building within him. The only available object close at hand was the steering wheel, so he made a fist and slammed and kept slamming. He was unable to stop himself until a sudden shooting pain starting from the tip of his fingers and extending to his elbow drew him up short. He screamed and grabbed onto his right elbow. He could not recall ever feeling so much pain in all his life.

He must have passed out from the pain, as the next thing he was aware of was the sound of loud banging. He slowly opened his eyes and tried to focus. As the fog lifted from his brain, he realized he was in his car and that someone was banging on the window. He soon recognized the face of Mr. Stevens, the superintendent of the building. He motioned for Luke to lower the window.

Luke struggled to a sitting position. He tried to speak but his mouth felt like cotton, and his head felt like someone had dropped a ton of bricks on it. "What time is it?" he mumbled.

"It's eight o'clock," replied Mr. Stevens.

"Morning or evening?" asked Luke.

"Morning," replied the superintendent, looking at him skeptically. Luke groaned and rubbed his eyes while attempting to get out of the car.

"Do you need help, Luke?" the superintendent asked.

Luke shook his head. Ignoring the pain in his arm, he replied, "No, I'm fine. Today is Monday, right?" he asked.

"Yes, it is," replied the superintendent.

Looking around, he couldn't believe it was Monday. *I can't believe I slept all night in my car,* he thought. He suddenly remembered he had to get to work, but he needed gas for his car.

"Do you have any gas I could borrow?" he asked Mr. Stevens. "I just need a little to get me to the station."

"Yes," replied Mr. Stevens. "Don't worry, I'll put it in for you."

Luke thanked him, handed over his car keys, and headed to his apartment to change his clothes. He winced as he attempted to remove his shirt. *I can't believe I hurt my arm that badly. How am I going to explain it to Mike? I need my right hand.*

It took him longer than he expected to change into clean clothes, as even the slightest movement caused him to groan as pain kept shooting up his arm. *I hope I can drive, or I'm going to be in big trouble*, he thought to himself.

With his one good arm, he managed to make it in to work, but not without great difficulty. Luckily, the cops were not on his route at that time of the day.

"I guess this is my lucky day," he told himself as he pulled into the parking lot. He was usually on time to open the office, but Mike had already done that.

"Luke, you're late," Mike called out as Luke entered the office.

"Sorry, Mike, I had a little accident." He held up his arm to show Mike his lower arm enveloped in a soft cast. "I had to go by the emergency room to get it looked at," he continued.

"What happened?" asked Mike, looking at his arm.

"Ah," Luke replied nonchalantly. "I just had a little mishap. It's so embarrassing, but my hand got caught in the car door. It's no big deal."

"Why didn't you call me? I would have picked you up," asked Mike.

Luke winced, remembering he had no phone. "My phone's not working," he lied.

"Will you be able to work? It's your right hand. How will you manage?" Mike asked with concern.

"I'll be fine, Mike. The doctor said it was just a very bad sprain. No bones are broken." Using his left hand, Luke started opening file cabinets and drawers, trying to convince Mike that he was able to do the work.

"Okay, as long as you can manage," Mike mumbled as he headed out to the garage.

Luke watched him go, thinking to himself, *I can't afford to take a day off. I need every dime I can get my hands on.*

35

It didn't take Luke a long time to heal, and within weeks he was back to his normal self. Finding Margaret remained at the top of his agenda. After all, it was almost two years now, and he was anxious to find out if she was still alive. The cast had been removed, but he still had some occasional discomfort in his hand, but he tried to be mindful of that and did all he could to avoid aggravating it. He had managed to steal and stash away a fair amount of cash, which he planned to use to find Margaret.

His priority this morning was to ramp up his Internet search. Having given it a lot of thought, he had decided to hire a private investigator, as all his other efforts had led to nothing but dead ends. He managed to do the minimum amount of office work then logged on to the Internet. After doing some search, he found what appeared to be a top-rated private investigator. His website, Pete Martin Investigations, Inc., was very impressive as were his credentials and client reviews. Luke decided he would call for an appointment. He was surprised when the call was answered by the PI himself. He was even more impressed that he was able to secure an appointment for later in the day. Before completing the conversation, he told Luke, "My office is being renovated. It's just a mess with dust everywhere. Can we meet at Lucky's restaurant? It's on Main and Bloor Streets, just down the street from your work address."

"Oh, sure. I can meet you at five," Luke replied.
"See you then," said Pete.

Luke entered the restaurant and allowed his eyes to adjust to the lighting. He had not met Pete Martin before, but based on the description he had given, Luke started walking toward the rear of the restaurant where he said he would be sitting. Suddenly he saw someone sitting at a booth beckoning toward him. As Luke approached, he realized that the man was trying to hide behind a menu. His face was partially obscured, so Luke had to look down in order to make eye contact with him.

"Are you Mr. Martin?" Luke asked.

"Oh, yes. You must be Luke? So nice to meet you." He stood up hurriedly and shook hands with Luke. "Have a seat, please. I'm Peter, everyone calls me Pete."

They both sat down, and Pete again resumed his previously odd behavior. Luke could not help himself; he had to say something. This man was acting too weird. He could not even see the man's face clearly.

"Excuse me, Pete, but are you okay? You're acting really weird. Why are you hiding behind the menu?"

"Well," replied Pete softly. "I'm actually working on a case, and I don't want to be seen. I don't want you to look now, or you'll blow my cover. Toward the front, second booth on the left, there's a woman who has been meeting with that man for a few weeks. Her husband asked me to do some surveillance on her, so that's why I have to be so careful." Luke nodded understandably while turning to see whom Pete was talking about. "Don't look now"—Pete hissed, still holding on to the menu—"or you'll ruin everything."

"Okay," replied Luke, opening his own menu.

"Are you ready to order?" They both looked up at the sound of the waitress.

"Yes, I'm ready," they both replied. They gave their orders, and the waitress left.

Luke decided to come straight to the point. "So, Pete, the reason I wanted to meet with you is to hire you to find my wife. She left almost two years ago, and I'm not sure where she is at the moment, but I'd really like to find her."

Pete looked at Luke. "First, I need to ask some questions before I decide if I'll take your case," Pete replied.

"Ask away," Luke replied, shrugging his shoulders. Pete pulled out a yellow legal pad from his briefcase and took notes as they talked.

"So, do you have a picture of your wife?" Pete asked.

Luke gave him a picture of Margaret. "This was taken about three years ago, so I don't know what she looks like now."

Pete took the picture and looked at it for a full minute. "Beautiful lady. I'll need to keep this," he replied. Luke nodded yes as Pete placed the picture in his briefcase.

"Did you contact the police when she first went missing?" Pete asked.

"No," replied Luke. "I thought she would return home after a while."

"Why did she leave home, Luke? Were you abusing her? Did you have another lady on the side?" Pete asked snidely.

Luke shifted uncomfortably in his seat. "Well, in every marriage there are disagreements. We were no different from other married couples."

"That might be true, Luke, but why did you wait almost two years before trying to find her?" asked Pete.

"Well, I kept hoping she would return. Matter of fact, I was involved in an accident and was hospitalized for quite some time. I just got my memory back, so that's why I'm just trying to find her," replied Luke.

Pete gave Luke a look that said, "I don't believe you for a minute." For a while, neither man spoke a word, both trying to size up the other.

Luke cleared his throat and finally asked, "So Pete, will you take my case? And how much will it cost?"

"Have you ever used a private investigator?" Pete asked.

"No," Luke replied.

"Well, this is how it all breaks down. There will be cost for my travel and hotel if I have to stay out of town overnight. There are also meals and other incidentals to be considered. Right now, we're not even sure which state she's in, so this might cost quite a bit. I charge an hourly rate. I will need a down payment from you tonight and the remainder as things move along. You seem like a nice guy, so I'm going to give you a very reasonable price." Pete smiled at Luke.

"Okay, that sounds fair. So how much are we talking about?" asked Luke anxiously.

"I'll take three to start," said Pete.

"Three hundred?" asked Luke.

Pete looked at Luke, trying his best not to laugh out loud. However, he couldn't help himself. "No, three thousand, Luke. You really know nothing about this business, do you?" he asked.

Luke was so surprised his mouth opened, but he had no words. Even though he had never used a PI before, never in his wildest dreams did he think that it would cost that much. After finding his voice, he was barely able to say, "That much?"

Pete looked him in the eye and smiled. "Yes, Luke, that's the deposit, and that's only because I like you."

Luke knew he didn't have anywhere near that amount on him, but he reached for his wallet anyway. He found three fifty-dollar bills plus one-hundred-dollar bill stashed in a secret compartment. He reluctantly removed this, as this was what he called his "rainy day money." Knowing he had no other money in his pocket, he kept searching anyway. He came up with only a few small bills, which he started counting. Pete was in no mood to wait, so he grabbed it from Luke's hand and counted them himself.

"This is only two fifty plus five singles," he said, looking at Luke.

"It's all I have," Luke said apologetically. "I didn't know you were going to ask for a down payment tonight."

Pete quickly pocketed the cash and looked at Luke. "Well, you owe me. When can you bring the rest?"

Luke pretended not to hear the question. "When will you start looking for her?" asked Luke.

"Very soon. You'll hear from me in about a week. I need some time to put out some feelers before I know which direction to go. If you don't hear from me, give me a call."

"Okay. Can I get a receipt for my down payment?" Luke asked.

Pete searched around in his briefcase. "Sorry, I just finished my old receipt book, and the new one is back at the office. I'll have it for you when you bring in the rest of your down payment. Is that all right?"

"Sure," Luke replied. "Will we meet here or at your office?"

"The repairs to my office should be finished by then, so we'll meet there. Here's my business card."

Luke accepted the card. "Nice card," he said to Pete.

Their meal arrived, but Luke had changed his mind. Pete had taken his last dime, so how would he pay for his meal? He stood up preparing to leave. "I'm sorry," he told the waitress. "I need to leave. Something just came up. Can you please cancel my order?" Not waiting for a reply, he looked at Pete who was busy with his meal and headed for the door.

For the next few days, Luke was on pins and needles waiting to hear some news from Pete. A week passed without a word, so Luke decided to call. The first call did not go through, so he waited until after lunch to call again. This time he received a recording that said the number was disconnected. "What? There must be some mistake," he said to himself.

He did not have the rest of the down payment, but he decided to stop by Pete's office on his way home anyway. He desperately needed to know how the search was going. He retrieved the business card Pete had given him and headed out. He was familiar with the name of the street but had never had a reason to drive in that direction before. He located the street without difficulty and kept an eye out for the number of Pete's office. He couldn't help but notice the condition of the buildings as he drove by. It appeared only a few were occupied, and they looked to be in desperate need of repairs. In fact, some of the buildings seemed to be abandoned and about ready to crumble. *Now why would a successful PI choose to have his office in this neighborhood?* Luke thought to himself as he drove on. He looked around for someone who might direct him to the address, but the street was deserted.

He drove down another block, thinking he must have made a wrong turn. He located the card and rechecked the address. No, he was on the right street. So he continued on, slowly looking at each number as he drove on. As he came to a vacant lot, he happened to notice a large billboard bearing the address he was looking for. He slowed to a crawl and then came to a complete stop as he read and reread the sign:

<blockquote>
For Sale by Owner
Prime location. 1.5 acres. Suitable for condominiums or town homes. Will build to specification. Call ——.
</blockquote>

Luke stopped reading. He had been taken!

36

Margaret had made an appointment for four o'clock to meet with a realtor. She was so excited at the thought of getting her own place she could scarcely contain her excitement. Time seemed to move slowly as she counted down the time for work to end.

Why does this always seem to happen? She wondered. *Whenever there's something exciting you need to do, time always seems to drag.* She smiled to herself as the thought entered her head. She had been very careful about saving her tips and paycheck and had bought only what was absolutely necessary. She had finally saved enough to start looking for her own place. What could be better than that?

At first she was reluctant to share her plans with Carol, hoping to surprise her after she had found the right place. But the more she thought about it, the more she felt it would be better to tell her before she started searching. After all, Carol had been so good to her; she did not want her to think that she was keeping secrets from her.

I think I should ask her to come with me, she thought to herself excitedly. Putting thought into action, she called Carol as soon as she had a break. Carol had the day off and had told Margaret she would be staying home to do her laundry and catch up on some reading.

"Carol," said Margaret excitedly as soon as Carol answered the phone. "Do you have any plans for this evening?" asked Margaret.

"No. Why?" asked Carol.

"Can you go somewhere with me? I'm sorry to ask at the last moment. I know I should have asked earlier, but…" Her voice trailed off.

"Well, I have no plans, but can I ask where we're going?"

"I'll tell you when I see you," said Margaret, still excited. "See you in a while." She hung up the phone.

Carol clicked off the phone, wondering what had gotten her friend so excited. "I guess I'll find out soon," she said to herself and went back to her reading.

Margaret's excitement remained with her all the way home. As soon as she entered the apartment, she blurted out, "I'm going to look at a condominium, that's what I wanted to tell you. I wasn't sure how you'd feel about it…" She was talking faster than she could form her words.

"Slow down, Margaret, slow down. Of course, I'm happy for you, and, of course, I'll come with you." She couldn't help but smile at Margaret's childlike excitement.

Margaret took a deep breath. "I'm glad you're okay with it," she said to Carol, smiling broadly. "I was worried you might think I was not grateful for all your help."

"Why wouldn't I be happy for you?" asked Carol, pulling her close and hugging her hard.

Lynn the realtor showed up on time as promised, and as they drove out of their neighborhood, Margaret was deep in thought, wondering about the new turn her life was about to take. She had never owned anything in her life, and now at age twenty-two, she was thinking of buying her own condominium.

How far I've come, she thought. *God has certainly blessed me.*

After a short ride, they entered a fairly new subdivision. The landscape looked as if it was lifted right off the pages of *Better Homes and Gardens* and deposited into the suburbs of Sycamore. It was attractive and well organized with not a scrap of garbage visible to mar its beauty. As they drove on, Margaret noticed that there were no more than six units grouped together. Lynn drove another short block then stopped in front of a row of units. Each unit had its own entrance and a small garden area in front. The smell of flowering plants was abundant in the air, and Margaret started thinking about the type of plants she would have in her new garden. They looked around before they entered. It was extremely quiet with only one person walking a small dog.

"It's so quiet," Carol said.

"It's so very clean," Margaret replied.

Lynn unlocked the door, and they entered. "This is the foyer," she said. "Notice how clean and spacious it is."

"Yes," replied Margaret. "I love the color of the walls, they're not too bold. I like it a lot."

"I thought you would," Lynn replied. "I kept in mind everything you told me about your preferences."

They continued down a short corridor passing a newly renovated kitchen, a powder room, a living room, and laundry room.

"This is so spacious," Margaret cried, walking into the living room.

"Oh, you can put your television right over the fireplace," said Carol. "And a nice sectional over there," she continued, pointing excitedly to a corner.

"Let's take a look at the bedrooms," Lynn said. They followed her upstairs, and soon they were looking at the larger of two rooms.

"This must be the master," Margaret squealed.

"Yes, it is," replied Lynn. "You can easily fit a king-size bed in here if you choose to."

"And this is the en suite," she continued, leading the way into the bathroom.

"The closet is so big," Carol said, still looking around the bedroom. "You'll need a lot of clothes and shoes to fill this closet," she laughed.

"That's not a problem," Margaret replied, laughing.

They returned downstairs, and Lynn led them to a door off the living room. "And now for the pièce de résistance," she said, leading them to a door located off the living room. She opened the door, and both Carol and Margaret walked onto a well-appointed balcony. The view from the balcony took both their breaths away.

"Margaret, this does it. If you don't want this condo, I'll take it. It's perfect," said Carol. They continued looking until they had covered the entire unit, and Margaret had seen everything she needed to see.

"Carol, what do you think?" asked Margaret, looking at her friend expectantly.

"I love it," replied Carol, still looking around. "When I'm not at my place, everyone will know where to find me," she said, laughing.

"I'm glad you like it. Your opinion is important to me." Margaret smiled.

"So can I start writing up a contract?" Lynn asked expectantly.

"I guess you can," replied Margaret. "I didn't think I'd like the first place I saw, but I feel good about this place, so I'm going for it. I only hope I'm making the right decision."

"I think you are," both Lynn and Carol said together. Everyone laughed as they headed back to Lynn's office.

Margaret had not bought a lot of household stuff while she was staying with Carol, so she had only her clothing and a few boxes of personal items to bring to her new place. Carol helped her move into her new condo a few days later. She had ordered new furniture, which would be delivered the following day, and she had to be there when they arrived. The new condo was not too far from Carols' place, so although she now had a new address, she had almost the same commuting time. She still had to pass by Carol's apartment on her way to the diner, so they continued traveling together.

"This worked out very well. It's like I never moved," laughed Margaret as she and Carol drove in to work.

"Yes, except that when I get home, you're not there," said Carol.

"Oh," Margaret rubbed Carol's back, choking up. "I don't know if I told you thanks for all you've done for me. I don't know if I'll ever meet another friend like you…" she sniffed.

Carol turned sideways, and looked at her affectionately. "Well, I hope you don't either. And yes, you've told me thanks a million times, and I've said 'you're welcome' a million times. However, I'll still miss you. Now stop crying before I start crying too."

They both laughed as Margaret pulled into the parking lot to start another hectic day at the diner.

37

As Luke read the sign on the billboard of the vacant lot, he felt as if his heart was being torn from his chest. He had lost almost all the money he had "borrowed" from Mike, and now he didn't know if he could ever afford to find Margaret.

"How could I allow myself to be duped?" he asked himself. He felt like a broken man. He headed for his apartment then changed his mind and drove to a nearby bar instead. He entered the dimly lit interior and took a stool at the farthest end of the bar. He was in no mood for conversation; all he wanted was to be alone to wallow and drown in his misfortune.

He wanted something to drink, and not just any drink. He wanted something as strong and maybe as dark as he felt. Soon the bartender approached to take his order. Luke looked up and growled, "Jamaican Wray and Nephew white rum on the rocks."

The bartender gave him a long look. "Are you sure? That is one-hundred-fifty-proof Jamaican rum. It's the strongest alcoholic drink on earth."

"You heard me. That's what I want," Luke replied.

"Okay, it's your funeral," replied the bartender, shaking his head as he went to get the order.

On the island of Jamaica, Wray and Nephew white rum is known as the "poor man's friend." An acquaintance of Luke's had once told him that this was absolutely the cheapest way of getting plastered, and at the moment that's what he wanted. He was a man who wanted to drown his sorrows, and right now white rum was his only friend.

"Not only have I given all my money to Pete the shuffler, but now he has disappeared. What else could go wrong?" he asked to no one in particular. The bartender placed his drink on the counter, folded his arms, and stood watching. Luke added a few drops of water to the glass and downed it all in one gulp.

He had no idea what hit him!

His heart started pounding, and his face took on the color of overripe strawberries. The hairs at the back of his neck stood erect, and his entire body felt as if engulfed in flames. As the alcohol burned its way down his throat and into his stomach, his eyes rolled backward in his head.

The eerie stillness of the bar was suddenly shattered as he grabbed his chest and yelled. "What a kick! Bartender, wherever that came from, get me another."

By the end of his third drink, Luke was ready to take on any- and everyone in the bar. Seeing two females sitting by themselves, he slid from the bar stool and staggered toward their table. He had always been a mean drunk, and today was no different.

"Ladies, you look…so beautiful. Can I…can I buy you a drink?" he slurred. Both women looked at him and started laughing. His speech had become more slurred and his balance increasingly unstable. As he drew closer to their table, he almost lost his balance. He tried to steady himself by grabbing on to the table. By now, all eyes were focused on him.

"This is not going to end well," said one patron to his drinking partner. Unable to regain his balance, the table began to tilt. Just as it was about to hit the floor, several male patrons rushed over to try and prevent an accident. Too late! The table clattered to the floor, spilling drinks over the female patrons and dousing Luke in the process. Luke's anger erupted.

No one knew for sure who took the first swing, but before long, a full-scale bar brawl was in progress. Tables, chairs, and fists went flying as people yelled and ducked. The bartender, not wanting to have the entire bar demolished, and his livelihood with it, quickly dialed 911. In no time, the police arrived. Looking around, the scene looked like an F4 tornado had descended on it.

Luke had no recollection of being brought to the police station. He slept the sleep of the dead. He woke up with a blinding headache, not the type he had ever experienced before. This was different. He felt like a herd of stampeding elephants were running through his head while his eyes felt like pebbles were engrained in them.

At first, his surroundings seemed unfamiliar. Realization finally dawned, and the first thing he saw were bars. In all his life, he had never been behind bars—not that he did not deserve to be! But so far he had been extremely lucky. "I hope my luck is not about to run out," he said, looking around fearfully. He was not alone in his cell! He had the good fortune of sharing it with two other occupants that looked as though they did not appreciate the noise. As fear descended, he shook the bars and yelled, "Officer, I need help!"

Luke had never felt this kind of fear before. All he wanted was to get as far from this place as possible. He wanted help, and fast, but fear prevented him from calling out again. Finally, a large African American officer with a clean-shaved head ambled toward him. Luke looked on in awe as this man-mountain made his way toward him. "What's all the noise about?" he asked.

Luke had to raise his head in order to see the officer's eyes, and even then he could barely see past his chest. At first all he could do was open his mouth and stare. He could not recall ever seeing anyone this large, and he had seen a lot during his short life.

The officer stared down at Luke. "I asked you what you wanted. The cat got your tongue?"

Luke shook his head as if waking from a trance. "I…I'm sorry," he stammered. "I just wanted to know when I'll get my phone call. Doesn't everyone get a free phone call?

The officer looked at him and smirked. "Yes, but as a rule, we don't wake drunks when they're brought in. We usually grant them the courtesy of letting them sleep it off." By now, Luke's headache had reached such unspeakable proportions all he wanted was relief.

"Can I have two aspirins, please?" he asked, holding onto his head.

"I thought you wanted to make a phone call?' asked the officer, walking away.

"Yes, please," whined Luke.

Mike was not happy about having to bail Luke out of jail. He paid the bail and headed back to his truck with Luke following meekly behind. All the way to his truck, Mike complained.

"I have never ever had to bail one of my employees from jail before. This is the first time, and I promise you this had better be the last!" he yelled at Luke. Mike's yelling just intensified Luke's headache, so he held onto his head with both hands covering his ears, trying his best to block out the sound.

"Yes, Mike. I'm truly, truly sorry. It won't happen again, I promise. Just stop yelling, please."

"You better believe it. Go home and sleep it off, you're in no condition to do any work today. I want to see you bright and early tomorrow. We'll talk about docking today's pay." Mike drove him back to the bar, where Luke gladly retrieved his car. He hurriedly made his escape to the quiet confines of his apartment and away from Mike's shouting.

38

Luke was in big trouble, and he knew it. Mike had been good enough to put up his bail after he had made his one phone call to him. He was definitely not looking forward to seeing him at work today. However, he knew if he wanted to keep his job, he had better show up for work. So as he slowly dressed, he kept thinking about what he could tell Mike to appease him.

Arriving at work, he managed to slink into the office without bumping into Mike.

"Thank God," Luke breathed as he realized there was no one else in the office. He was on time; matter of fact, he was earlier than usual. He really wanted to try and get back in Mike's good graces. He knew if he lost this job, he would be in serious trouble. Things were busy in the garage judging from the noise coming from that area. He made himself look busy; he did not want Mike thinking he was a slacker, not after what he had done for him. He owed Mike big time.

"I see you're back. Are you okay?" said a voice behind him. Luke almost jumped out of his skin.

"Mike, I didn't hear you come in. Yes, I'm okay. Thanks again for your help."

"You're welcome." Mike took a seat behind the desk and started to say something then changed his mind. He looked at

Luke, pulled on his cigar, then headed for the garage. He turned as if he had forgotten something.

"Luke, I hope you're ready to put in some hard work to make up for yesterday. I want you to get the books together. My accountant is coming over later this week to take a look. He wants to make sure I'm not stealing from the IRS. I'm sure you have everything in order. I told him he'll be meeting with you, as you're the one handling the money." He laughed heartily at the thought. "Imagine me stealing from the IRS." He continued laughing and shaking his head as he closed the door and headed to the garage.

Luke turned as white as a ghost. Luckily, Mike had already left the office, or he would have thought that Luke was on the verge of fainting. He quickly sat down before he fell down. His heart sped up as he realized the magnitude of what was about to happen. He would be sent to jail, and all because he had been too greedy.

"It's over. I've got to get out of here. I can't go to jail," he said to himself, anxiety overriding sanity. He was nervous, but he couldn't afford to show it, so he tamped it down and went about his work as usual. It was the longest day of his life! Where would he go? What would he do?

He began gathering the papers that would be needed by the accountant: records on each customer transaction, receipts, and bank deposit slips. He wasn't sure about the accounts receivable because his accounting system was not the best, and some of the receipts had been misplaced. What he could find, he placed in a legal-size envelope and placed it on the desk. Half the cash that he had collected that day was placed in the night deposit bag and then in the file cabinet, as he had no intention of going to the bank. The other half he placed into his pocket.

"I'll need some cash, I can't leave with empty pockets," he told himself. Shortly before closing time, he stopped and looked around. He felt very sad. This had not been a bad place to work after all. "I'll miss this place. I'm sorry it did not work out, Mike.

I'm sorry I disappointed you, and that it had to end this way," he said to the empty room.

He thought about writing a letter to Mike, but what would he say? "Sorry, you shouldn't have trusted me?" He took one long look, turned the lights off, and headed for his car. He made it home to his apartment in record time and took the stairs two at a time. He quickly stuffed some clothes and personal items into a large duffel bag, took one last look around the apartment, and almost lost it.

"I really loved this place," he said. "Unfortunately, I have no choice but to go." With one last look, he headed out the door. He had no idea where he was headed; all he knew was that he had to get as far away as possible from the town of New Hope.

39

Luke took the highway north out of town thinking his luck might be better in a northern state. His mind was in a constant state of turmoil, and as darkness fell, he started thinking about where he would sleep. He didn't want to waste his money on motels; he would need it for food and gas. The next best thing would be to sleep in his car at one of those truck stops; at least he would be safe there for one night. No one would realize what he had done until the next day, so the best thing would be to keep going and get as far away from New Hope as possible.

The road was dark and lonely, and Luke caught himself nodding off a few times. But as tired as he was, he figured he would push himself while it was still dark until he could go no further. Tomorrow would be a different day and a different story. Right now he needed something to eat as he had not eaten since lunch.

"I'll stop by the next truck stop and get something from the vending machine," he told himself.

Summer was fading fast, and already the night had that undeniable feeling of coolness, reminding everyone that autumn was not far away. To help him stay awake, Luke opened the window and breathed in the cool fresh air. The radio was turned up to maximum to keep him company. Soon he spotted a truck stop and pulled off. The area was crowded with tractor trailers, trucks, and a few cars. Only a few people were in sight. He parked in an area where it was difficult to be spotted.

"I guess everyone has turned in for the night," he said to himself as he slowly emerged from his car, stretching as he did. He was stiff and a bit sore, and his muscles rebelled from the long period of inactivity. The red neon arrow pointing to the restroom was a welcome sight, so he picked up speed and headed in that direction as fast as his legs could take him. By the time he exited the restroom, his stomach was making hunger noises, so he had no choice but to pay attention. The vending machines consisted of the usual fare—chips, pretzels, crackers, and soda. This was not what he wanted, but tonight he was a beggar, and beggars could not be choosers.

As he greedily munched on the stale chips, he could not remember tasting anything so good. It was like manna from heaven. Instead of buying water from the machine, he returned to the restroom, cupped his hands under the faucet, and drank until his thirst was fully quenched.

Returning to his car, he decided it was as good a time as any to get some sleep. He climbed into the backseat and tried his best to get comfortable. Using some of the clothes he had hastily thrown on the backseat, he covered himself, and in no time flat, he was sound asleep.

40

Luke awakened to the rumbling of truck engines. It was still dark, but he could see in the distance that daylight was not too far off. After gently extricating himself from his cramped quarters, he started working on some stretches to remove the kinks from his neck and shoulders. Every joint in his body seem to ache, but he continued stretching until the last vestige of pain disappeared, and circulation gradually returned.

"I don't care. I have to find a cheap motel tonight and get some decent sleep," he said to himself. He added gas to his car then returned to the vending machines for some coffee. At the first sip, he made a face and spat out the first mouthful. It was the worst-tasting coffee he had ever tasted in his life. It was cold, stale and just plain putrid.

"What did they use to make this?" he asked. "I've never tasted diesel oil, but this must be what it tastes like." As badly as he wanted some coffee, he could not bring himself to take another sip, so he threw the contents in the grass and went back to the restroom to rinse his mouth and freshen up.

"I have to be very careful today," he told himself as he prepared to pull out from the rest stop. "It won't be long before my deeds will be brought to light."

The sign on the highway told him he was still in New York state, and just another fifty miles and he would cross into Connecticut.

"I think I'll stay in Connecticut for a while," he said to himself as he drove. "Maybe a different state is just what I need for my luck to start changing." He made sure he stayed within the speed limit so as not to attract any unwanted attention, especially that of the highway police. Glancing at the clock on the dashboard, it showed a little after 8:00 a.m. His hunger had not been satisfied from the vending machine fare, so finding a diner was at the top of his to-do list.

Mike should be opening up the office soon, he thought to himself. *I'm so sorry, Mike. You didn't deserve this, but what else could I do?*

Luke was not the smartest person alive, but he was sure that someone was going to be looking for him before long. His original plan was to drive as far as he could while it was still dark and lie low during daylight. However, today was an exception, and as soon as he found a quiet little town, he would get something to eat and rest up until dark before moving on. There were no houses visible from the highway, and traffic was very sparse, and he soon forgot his hunger and started to enjoy the beautiful landscape flying by.

"These are some beautiful views," he said as he drove on. "It must be nice living in the country."

He was never one to take the time to enjoy the beauty of nature; he was always too busy. But despite his present situation, he could not help himself. The leaves had just started changing color, heralding the onset of autumn. They were all on display, abundant in all their glory as far as the eyes could see.

Born and raised in the city, Luke had seen the beauty of the fall season before, but nothing on such a magnificent scale. It was as if Mother Nature had decided to spread a blanket of her most treasured colors for everyone to see and enjoy. His stomach kept reminding him that it had been some time since he had had a decent meal, and he could no longer ignore the call.

He decided to heed the call and take the next exit. Soon a sign flew by informing him that the Chastain exit was coming up, and soon it came into view. Luke decided he would get some more gas and something to eat.

"Chastain…such a nice name," he said to himself as he positioned himself to take the exit ramp. A sign indicated that the nearest diner was located half a mile from the highway. As he pulled up to the diner, he couldn't help but notice how quiet the town was. There were very few cars parked out front, and even fewer patrons on the inside. He took a seat at the counter and was soon approached by a waitress.

"Hello, handsome. What can I get for you?" she asked, smiling.

"What do you have that I'd like?" asked Luke, taking her question as a come-on.

The waitress pointed to the menu. "It's almost lunch time, but we serve breakfast all day. Take your time and let me know when you're ready to order." She walked away to attend to another customer. Luke busied himself with the menu, totally unaware of the police officer that was taking more than a passing interest in his car.

41

Chastain was a small town, and as small towns go, nothing or no one new went unseen by the residents or the keepers of the law in a town this small. Luke was about to place his order when another patron entered the diner. No one turned to see who it was, but that sixth sense we all possess went into overdrive. Luke felt prompted to turn around to see who was standing in his aura. He paled as his heart performed a series of flip-flops. *Mike turned me in. I thought I'd have a bit more time. Freedom as I know it is over*, he thought to himself.

Doing his best to control his anxiety, he cleared his throat and said as calmly as he could, "Hello, Officer."

The officer took his time returning the greeting. "Good morning, sir. Passing through town, are you?"

"Yes, sir," Luke replied calmly. The last thing he wanted to do was to antagonize the officer, so he tried to be on his best behavior.

"May I see an ID? Make that your driver's license, registration, and insurance, please," said the officer.

"Of course, officer," replied Luke, reaching for his wallet. He produced the driver's license and registration as requested by the officer.

The officer returned to his car to verify the legitimacy of the documents then returned. He looked at Luke to compare the likeness. Satisfied with the similarity of the picture ID and the person standing before him, he returned the license to Luke.

"My insurance card is in my car," he told the officer.

The officer made no response. "Where are you heading, Mr. Foster?" the officer asked. Luke's mind raced as he thought hard of the name of a town in Connecticut. Suddenly the name "Hartford" popped into his head, and he latched on to it. Appearing ignorant or anxious was the last thing he wanted, so putting on his most respectable face, he replied, "I'm going to Hartford, sir."

Again the officer took his time before responding. "Where are you coming from?" asked the officer.

"New Hope, sir." Luke replied.

"Do you have family in Hartford?" the officer continued.

Luke was now becoming angry at the interrogation, so before the officer could ask another question, he asked. "Did I do something wrong, Officer? I just came in to get some breakfast, and here you are interrogating me as if I was some common criminal. Now if you have nothing further to ask, and I'm not under arrest, then I'll be on my way, thank you."

Not waiting for a response, Luke slammed out of the diner, and without adding gas to his car, he headed back to the highway.

He gave a sigh of relief as he entered the highway and saw that it was free and clear. "That was way too close for comfort," he said to himself as he started to relax. But no sooner had his shoulders returned to its normal relaxed position than the sound of a police siren pierced the silence of the autumn air. Taking one look in his rearview mirror, Luke saw the flashing blue light of a police car fast approaching. He had no idea if they were coming after him, but he was not about to wait around to find out. His foot hit the gas pedal, and the car sprang forward.

"Okay, show me what you've got!" Luke shouted as the speedometer skyrocketed.

Before long, the lights from the police car started to recede, and Luke decided he was no longer safe on the highway. He reverted to his original plan of lying low during the day and driving only at night. Seeing an unpaved road, he decided to take his chances and see where it would lead. He exited the highway and parked under some thick foliage. He was not visible from the highway, especially not by the police cruiser that soon went flying by.

Luke sat quietly in his car looking at his surroundings and enjoying the beauty of his surroundings. Suddenly his stomach rumbled, a stark reminder that he had missed breakfast again. He got out of his car and started looking around. He was surrounded by rolling green pastures dotted with Black Angus cows all feeding contentedly on the luscious green grass. In adjoining paddocks were large numbers of beautiful horses of all size and colors. He leaned against the railing, enjoying the sight of the young foals and fillies scampering around without a care.

He sighed. "Welcome to God's country," he said to himself.

42

Margaret was happier than she had ever been in a very long time. Summer was on its way out, and she was looking forward to enjoying the beauty of the fall foliage. Her life had taken such an amazing direction; she never could have envisioned it even in her wildest dream. She was so engulfed in her daily life that all thoughts of Luke Foster had gradually receded to the back of her mind.

She was deriving so much pleasure from decorating her new apartment that she looked forward to each new day. Each time she went on her regular neighborhood jaunts, she would discover some new treasure. She was such a familiar sight at the local antique stores that many of the vendors knew her by name.

"I'm in no hurry to fill this apartment," she told herself. "I have all the time in the world." And so it was, like a mother hen gathering her chicks, she lovingly began gathering unique pieces that could not fail to catch the eye of all who came to visit her.

At the end of her shift, Margaret hurriedly changed from her uniform into her street clothes. Carol was going shopping with her for a change and could not help but notice her excitement.

"You really enjoy visiting these antique stores, don't you?" asked Carol.

Margaret's face lit up. "Yes, I do. I'm so glad you're coming with me today. I want you to see the large variety of merchandise they carry. They have all these beautiful vases, silverware, mirrors…whatever you need, it's there, and the quality is so—"

Carol interrupted before she ran out of breath. "Okay, okay, I believe you," said Carol, laughing. "The last time I visited your place, I could tell that you really have an eye for beautiful things. I love the way your condo's shaping up."

"I would never be able to afford the stuff I have if I had to buy them brand new," said Margaret.

Traffic was moving at a rapid pace as they exited the diner's parking lot, and so in no time, they reached the small strip mall where the antique dealers were located. Judging from the number of cars in the parking lot, it seemed they were doing a thriving business. As they entered the confines of the store, Carol looked on in amazement at the large number of stalls. Everywhere she looked there were nothing but merchandise of all shapes, sizes, and description.

"My goodness, I had no idea this place was even here," Carol said, looking around with eyes wide open. "Come on, let's go shopping," she said, grabbing hold of a cart and picking up speed. Margaret ran to keep pace with her.

"Slow down," she said, laughing out loud. "They're opened until ten o'clock. We have at least five hours."

Carol slowed down, and they took their time perusing each booth, choosing unusual finds and placing them in their cart. They finally came to one booth where Margaret had previously bought a number of rare figurines. Recognizing Margaret, Anna, the booth's owner, called out. "Hi, Margaret. I see you've brought your friend today."

"Hi, Anna. This is Carol," Margaret replied. "I've told her all about you and the wonderful, unusual things you have."

"Welcome, Carol," replied Anna. "Take your time and browse. Let me know what speaks to your heart today." They took their time browsing between booths, selecting and then rejecting several items, each piece looking nicer that the other. "Everything looks so nice I have a hard time making up my mind," said Carol in mock frustration.

"Don't worry," replied Margaret. "I felt the same when I first started coming here. After a while, you'll know what really speaks to you, and you'll know exactly what to buy and what not to."

Time flew by, and still they continued shopping. Spying a pair of ornate silver candlesticks, Carol picked them up. "I know exactly where I'll put this," she said, looking at the price. "I can't believe this is all they cost," she said with eyes opened wide while looking at Margaret.

"Are you taking them? Because if you don't, I will," replied Margaret, smiling.

"Oh no, you won't," replied Carol, quickly placing them in the cart. Suddenly she laughed and held on to her stomach, which had started rumbling in protest.

"What time is it?" she asked, looking at her watch. "Oh my goodness, it's almost ten. They'll be closing soon," she said, looking at Margaret. "No wonder my stomach was making hunger noises. We'd better head for the checkout." They pushed their loaded cart to the checkout and were amazed at the small amount they had to pay. They hurried to the car to stash their precious finds.

"I can't believe all these lovely things I got for so little money," Carol said in awe.

"I told you," replied Margaret. "Let's get something to eat before we head home."

"I'm all for that," replied Carol, wrapping her jacket around her to stave off the cold. They headed for the nearest restaurant.

43

"Chinese buffet. Mm, my favorite!" exclaimed Carol as they headed for the restaurant located at the other end of the mall.

"I think I can eat just about everything in sight," replied Margaret. Soon they were settling into a booth, their plates almost overflowing. They remained quiet as they enjoyed all the variety the buffet had to offer. After returning to the tables for refills a few times, they were finally sated. Holding on to her stomach, Carol gasped. "I couldn't eat another bite if you paid me."

"Same here," replied Margaret. "We'd better get going. We have work in the morning, plus I have a class in the evening."

Margaret dropped Carol off at her apartment and headed for her condominium. "I'm too tired to unload my purchases tonight," she said to herself. "I'll do that tomorrow." She had just enough energy left to take a shower and flop into bed before she started snoring.

As she headed into work the following morning, Margaret realized she had not unpacked her treasures from shopping the evening before. "I'll unpack after work," she told herself before driving off to pick up Carol for the daily ride to the diner. No sooner had the diner doors opened than they were swamped with hungry customers. As soon as the breakfast crowd vacated the diner, things got underway preparing for the lunch crowd. Neither one had a chance to take a break until it was almost the end of their shift.

"Oh, my feet," Margaret moaned, sitting in a chair and massaging her feet. "I feel as if they're going to fall off."

"You're not alone," replied Carol, collapsing onto the nearby couch. They had a quick bite to eat, and soon it was back to the grindstone for both.

On their way home, Carol asked, "Are you going back to the antique store?"

"No way. I still haven't unpacked my car from last night," replied Margaret. "I also have a class this evening, remember? In addition, I don't plan on going back there until the end of the month. What are you planning to do?"

"I'm planning to catch up on my sleep—after I have a long, warm foot soak," sighed Carol contentedly.

College was proving to be quite a challenge for Margaret. When you throw full-time work, class work, and volunteering into the mix, it can prove to be quite a handful. Her ability to manage her school work was never in doubt, but you can push a body but so far and no further. Margaret was extremely intelligent, but with the physical demands of work, she had no choice but to push herself to keep up with her assignments. She often looked back with regret that she had not gone straight to college right after high school.

But as she told herself more than once, "I was young then and free from responsibilities. I should have gone to college then. But as the saying goes, 'I made my bed. I guess I'll just have to sleep in it.'"

After a short nap, she woke with a start, thinking she had overslept. Feeling far from refreshed, she felt compelled to do some stretches to remove the kinks from her body, but the tiredness persisted. She dragged herself to the bathroom thinking a hot shower would help, but one glance at the clock told her there was not enough time. Almost at a run, she hurriedly collected her books and headed for her car.

"I hope I can stay awake in class," she yawned as she settled in and buckled and adjusted her seatbelt. It was literally a crawl from the moment she hit the main street. "All the stoplights seemed to be working against me today," she said as she stopped for yet another red light.

She jumped as the blaring of a car horn bombarded her senses. Realizing she had fallen asleep, she stepped on the accelerator and just barely missed slamming into the car ahead of her. With adrenaline surging through her body, she stayed awake until she pulled into a parking space in the college parking lot.

"A cup of coffee would certainly hit the spot right now, but I'm running late," she said, increasing her steps. Her current professor was a stickler for time and always started classes on the dot. She barely made it to her seat before the lecture started. More than once she had to shake herself awake as she felt herself drifting off. Some people might say that sleep is overrated, but sleep was a powerful thing, and before long she was in dreamland.

"Ms. Foster, are you still with us?"

Margaret jumped at the sound of her name. The eyes of everyone, including Professor King, was focused on her. Realizing she had drifted off to sleep, she quickly apologized. "I'm sorry."

"I know you're all tired," the professor replied sympathetically. "Evening classes are usually very tiring, as most of you have jobs and families. But I want you to get as much as possible from this class."

Margaret fought hard to stay awake the remainder of class, but it was a challenge. She observed other classmates nodding off in class before and was glad to know she was not the only one struggling to get a higher education.

44

Luke soon tired of the scenery, and with no place in sight to get a meal, he returned to his car. He scrounged around and soon discovered an old Snickers bar hidden under the seat. It looked old and raggedy, didn't smell all that good either, but he could not afford to be choosy, so he ate heartily, not knowing when he would be able to get a decent hot meal. He felt safe and comfortable hidden under the thick foliage, and his plan was to hunker down there for the rest of the day.

The weather remained cool, and all he had was a light coat. He had been using his extra clothing for warmth so far, but he knew he would have to buy a warm coat as soon as he had a chance. "How could I forget to throw in my heavy jacket?" He asked himself with regret. His inactivity was starting to make itself felt, so he put on an extra shirt, wrapped his light coat around him, switched the heater on, and before long he drifted off to sleep.

He was sound asleep one minute; the next he was rudely awakened by someone banging on the window of his car. *This is becoming a habit*, he thought angrily to himself and settled in and made himself a bit more comfortable. The loud banging continued, and soon sleep deserted him. He slowly opened his eyes. To his surprise, he was staring down the barrel of a gun aimed directly at his head.

Luke blinked and hesitated, trying to get his bearings. He looked around only to see that he was surrounded by a crowd. In addition to a number of people, there were several farm animals all encircling his car and staring at him. Though only half-awake, the situation appeared so comical he wanted to laugh. But with a cop pointing a gun at his head, he knew that was the worst thing he could do. It was just not the right time, and so he sat still, gathering his thoughts. Luke recognized the officer who had accosted him at the diner earlier, and this knowledge only served to raise his ire.

The veteran officer had seen that hesitant behavior many times and knew the only thing on the mind of the potential suspect was how to escape his present situation. The officer took better aim and commanded, "Don't even think about it, son. It won't end well for you. Get out with your hands up."

Luke realized that for now there was no escape, so he unlocked the car door and stepped out.

The sequence of events were never quite clear. One minute the officer was placing the handcuffs on Luke's wrists, and the next minute there was the sound of gunshot. Luke looked down; the officer was lying on the ground bleeding. The small crowd was dumbfounded, unable to believe what had just happened. The farmer, his two sons, and a farmhand started backing away slowly as Luke, with the officer's gun in hand, looked from one to the other. Quickly summing up the situation, he took charge. Pointing to the smallest person of the group, he asked, "What's your name?"

"Liam," the boy answered nervously.

"Is that your dad?" Luke asked, pointing to the older man in the group. The boy nodded yes, sidling up closer to his dad. "How old are you?" Luke asked.

"Twelve," the boy answered. He appeared small, short, and skinny for his age. You could see the fear written on his young face.

Pointing to some rope lying nearby, Luke ordered, "Get over there and bring that rope." The boy did as he was told. He tried handing the rope to Luke, but this was not exactly what Luke had in mind. Using the gun, Luke pointed to the older man. "Go tie him up."

"He's my dad. I can't do that," Liam answered fearfully.

"If you don't, I promise I'll have to shoot him," replied Luke.

Tears started gathering in young Liam's eyes. He looked hesitantly at his father, silently asking what to do. His father nodded at him, "Do what he tells you, son. It's okay."

"But, D-dad…" he stuttered.

"It's okay, Liam. Do what the man says," his father encouraged him.

Luke smiled a cold, hard smile. "That's right, and make it snappy."

Liam reluctantly tied the hands of his father, apologizing as he did what Luke commanded. Liam's brother, Seth, and the farmhand, Steve, received the same treatment until Liam and Luke were the only two remaining free and standing.

"Come over here, Liam. You've been an obedient boy." Luke smiled as the boy walked toward him. He put his arm around the boy's shoulder and gave him a friendly squeeze. Liam cringed as he tried extricating himself from Luke's grasp.

"What do you think I should do with you, Liam?" he asked.

The boy shrugged. "I don't know," he replied, tears hovering on his lashes then running down his face.

"Would you like to come with me?" asked Luke.

"No, I don't want to go anywhere with you," replied Liam angrily, still trying to loosen Luke's grip on his arm.

"Oh, that's too bad. I thought we could be friends."

Liam glared at him, the tears still running down his face. Walking over toward the three men now lying next to each other, Luke called out.

"Gentlemen, I guess this is good-bye. It was nice while it lasted, but unfortunately, all good things must come to an end. You've all been such good company that I hate to leave. However, I have a little something for you to remember me by."

Ending his little speech, he walked closer to the men. He lifted his right foot and one by one aimed it at the ribs of all three. The sound of breaking bones was audible as the toe of Luke's heavy boot connected with the rib cage of each man. Their response was not unexpected as each man cried out, a reaction to the incredible pain that was radiating throughout their bodies.

"*No!*" Liam screamed as he ran toward his family all hurt and lying on the ground writhing in pain. He tried lifting his dad by the shoulders as he curled up in pain. Unable to lift him, he hugged his dad while looking up at Luke, his eyes filled with hate. "Why did you do that? They did nothing to hurt you," cried Liam.

Luke gave him a hard look. "Liam, sometimes in life, you can't wait for someone to hurt you first."

Liam released his hold on his father and moved toward Luke, both tiny fists curled as tight as he could muster. He took a running leap and started raining down blows on Luke. He didn't care where they landed; all he wanted to do was hurt this man who had hurt his family. Luke swatted him like a pesky fly, but Liam was determined and kept on coming. Finally, he landed one blow in the area of Luke's family jewels. Luke saw stars as he doubled over in pain.

Liam finally backed away, pleased with himself that at least one blow had connected with the right spot. "That'll show you!" he yelled.

"And I'll show you," shouted Luke as he limped over toward Liam, gun in hand. One blow from the butt of the gun to Liam's head, and Liam fell, sprawled on the ground, unmoving.

Luke limped away, one hand on his groin, the other holding the gun. He cared not that it was still light out; he had to get away from this place. He slowly climbed into his car, reversed onto the dirt road, careful to avoid the officer lying bleeding on the ground. He hit the highway and headed north with never a backward glance.

45

The police car remained parked on the farmer's dirt road. The car radio kept up a steady chatter, but there was no one to answer. The three men remained on the ground, groaning from the pain that had been inflicted on them. Luckily, Liam had not been strong enough to secure the ropes tightly, so Steve, the farmhand, was able to work his hands free. He struggled to stand, groaning with each movement. Taking each breath proved a monumental task, but he was determined to help his family. He soon had the rope loosened on each one, but unfortunately, Liam remained unconscious.

"We need to call for help," David, the father, said breathlessly. "Seth, do you have your cell phone?" Seth shook his head no, and so did Steve.

"We need to figure out how to use the radio in the police car," the father continued. The three slowly made their way to the police car, each one holding on to his side and to each other, groaning with each step. Seth was the most tech savvy of the three and soon figured out how to use the radio. Soon they were connected with the police dispatcher.

"We've been attacked. We need help." David stopped and took a shallow breath before continuing. "One of your officers is here. He's been shot." There was a sharp intake of breath on the line, but soon a very composed voice returned. "Did you say one of our officers has been shot, sir?

"Yes, replied David.

"Where are you calling from, sir?"

"The Whelan farm off Route 18. We're on the dirt road where the pastures are located."

"Is the officer breathing, sir?" asked the operator.

"I don't really know, but he has lost a fair amount of blood," the farmer replied.

"Are you alone, sir?" the dispatcher continued.

"No, there are four of us plus the officer. We're all hurt, and my youngest son is on the ground just barely breathing. Send some ambulances, please," David pleaded.

"Don't worry, sir. Police and ambulances are on their way," the operator replied. Barely able to take another breath, David whispered, "Thank you, thank you." As the last words escaped his lips, the phone slipped from his hands, and he slowly slumped to the ground.

Despite all that had recently transpired, Luke was surprisingly calm. His primary intention after leaving the farm was to get off the main thoroughfare to a road less frequently traveled. His final destination was still unclear, but one thing was quite clear—if caught, he was not going without a fight.

"Well, this was not planned," he said, trying hard to justify what had just transpired. "Not only am I a thief, now I'm a murderer—a cop killer, no less. That means the electric chair, and I'm way too young to die."

The car radio was on, but Luke's mind was way too busy with other things. Listening to the radio was the last thing on his mind. He was now a fugitive on the run.

46

Police cars from all the neighboring precincts had now converged on the Whelan farm. The staccato chatter from their radios seemed to be in competition with the tractors and the barking dogs. The sounds of approaching ambulances and fire trucks served to add to the ongoing chaos. As they skidded to a halt in the dirt-covered field, a fine covering of dust seemed to rise up to welcome them.

The scene confronting the officers was enough to raise the ire of any law-abiding person. They surveyed the scene, their anger rising minute by minute. It was clear that their police brother was in big trouble, and whoever was responsible for this carnage was going to pay big time when caught.

The EMTs hurried over to examine the injured officer. One look at him, and the EMTs knew his condition was critical. His color was pale and ashen, and his skin cold and clammy. Every breath he took was followed by a spray of bright-red blood on exhalation. He was gently positioned onto his back while an endotracheal tube was inserted into his lungs to help him breathe. He had lost a lot of blood, and temporarily replacing it with IV fluids was crucial to restore fluid and electrolytes.

EMTs are usually experts at starting IVs, so Brad, the first EMT, reached for his emergency bag and collected the items he needed to start an IV.

In some patients, veins can sometimes be difficult to locate, as was the case with this officer, but this was not unexpected. Using the largest-bore needle he could find, Brad palpated the inner aspect of the elbow, but locating a vein was proving to be a challenge. This was not unusual. Brad knew that whenever there was large amount of blood loss, there was going to be a drop in blood pressure, resulting in a collapse of some veins. However, he was up for the job, and after some additional searching, he located a vein by the side of the officer's neck. He gave a quick wipe with an alcohol swab and inserted the needle.

"This site is not as clean as I would like," Brad murmured to himself. "But time is of the essence. Antibiotics will take care of any infection…if he survives." The needle entered the vein easily, but the blood return was sluggish in entering the hub of the needle. However, Brad was not deterred. He attached the IV tubing and opened the valve as wide as possible. The fluids ran sluggishly at first then picked up speed and ran in unhindered. Brad released a breath he didn't even know he was holding and went in search of another vein.

Carl, the other EMT had his own set of problems trying to control the massive bleeding from the officer's chest. Despite the pressure being applied, the bleeding was not abating. The task was a difficult one, and as experienced as he was, he knew the outcome could be grim if things did not start improving. After what seemed like a lifetime applying pressure to the area, the blood started to clot, and the flow started to subside.

"With the amount of blood surrounding his body, it's difficult to see where the bullet entered and exited. Let's turn him on his side," Carl suggested to Brad.

Together they moved him onto his side. The entry site of the wound was now visible, and bright-red blood started gushing from the opening. The officer was completely unconscious and incapable of assisting, so this was solid dead weight, and the effects was starting to tell on both their backs.

"Some help over here, please," Carl yelled, barely able to keep holding on to the solid weight. Three officers ran over to help. "Put some gloves on," Brad yelled to one officer, indicating a box of latex gloves nearby. They quickly donned gloves, and together they supported their wounded comrade on his side.

"Press as hard as you can," Brad instructed one officer, handing him a bundle of gauze dressings. He applied pressure to the area until the amount of bleeding had reduced to a slight oozing.

This is as stable as he's going to get, Carl thought to himself, but he would never say this out loud. Instead, he said to his partner, "Brad, it's time to move."

Brad was thinking the same thing. "Yes, let's do it," he replied. The other officers came forward, and together they assisted with transferring him safely onto the gurney then into the ambulance. The paramedics jumped in, and with tires squealing and siren's blaring, they barreled out of the farm and onto the highway, heading for St. John's Trauma Center, the nearest hospital emergency room.

Not a dry eye could be found among those burly police officers, all angry that one of their own had been mowed down while performing his sworn duty. They quickly followed behind the ambulance, determined that if one of them was going to die, he would not die alone. They would be present en mass to show support and brotherhood to one of their own.

47

No words were spoken as the caravan of police cars, all with flashing lights and blaring sirens, followed the ambulance to the emergency room. They parked their patrol cars wherever space was available. The ER staff had been alerted about their imminent arrival and was ready and waiting. The staff had seen their share of traumas many times over, especially of police officers; but it never failed to strike a sensitive cord in the hearts of many since more than a few of the nurses were married to police officers themselves.

Dr. Isaac Martin was the assigned police surgeon on duty. His job was to render care to all police officers entering the emergency room. He was also responsible for examining and treating all members of the police force for injuries and illnesses they sustained in the line of duty. Waiting with Dr. Martin was a trauma surgeon, a neurosurgeon, and an orthopedic surgeon. Other specialists were on call, to be contacted as needed. An initial assessment was done and a chest tube quickly inserted into his lungs to prevent collection of blood and fluid while keeping the lungs inflated. The officer was then whisked off to the Operating Room.

As soon as he entered the OR, the required identification process was quickly attended to, and then the major task of trying to save his life got underway. The x-rays that were done on arrival showed that the bullet had entered the middle lobe of the officer's left lung and was lodged not far from his heart.

After a quick skin prep, the surgeons opened and entered the officer's chest, noting the damage done by the bullets from the Smith & Wesson M&P 9 handgun. The damage was more severe than had been anticipated.

"The mid lobe is completely gone," said Dr. Martin, examining the lung fragments in his hands.

"The upper lobe is damaged also," replied Dr. Henry, the pulmonologist. They searched around and finally located the bullet, which they removed and placed aside for evidence.

The entire operative procedure lasted for four grueling hours. Dr. Martin exited the operating room, a fluid-resistant gown covering his once sterile cloth OR scrubs. He headed for the waiting room where family and a group of officers were anxiously waiting. As he entered the room, he was quickly surrounded by both family members and police officers. They bombarded him with questions.

"How is he, Doc?" they asked as they crowded around, anxious for any information they could get.

Doctor Martin raised his hands for calm. "Take it easy, everyone. Let me tell you what I know, and then I'll try to answer your questions the best way I can. At the moment, Officer Harvey is in the surgical Intensive Care Unit. He is very critical but stable. It was touch and go for a while, but he came through. I cannot make any promises as he lost a lot of blood, but I'm hoping for the best."

"Did you remove the bullet doc?" asked one officer.

"Yes, we were able to remove the bullet with a lot of difficulty because of where it was lodged. I'm sure you'll want that for evidence."

"When can we see him?" another officer asked.

"Not anytime soon. As I said, he's very critical, and he's unconscious and on a breathing machine. He wouldn't be able to recognize or communicate with you anyway." They continued crowding around him as if his nearness could relieve their anxiety and bring them the good news they so desperately craved. Their eyes quietly demanded more answers, which they knew were not coming, but that did not stop them from hoping. So much raw emotion was visible on their faces; it almost broke Dr. Martin's heart. Watching tears welling in their eyes, he fought hard to control his own emotions as he prepared to leave the room. "Now if there are no more questions, I'll leave…"

"Just one more question, Doc," a deep voice called out from the rear of the room. Dr. Martin stopped in his tracks. As he looked, a large Herculean officer with the softest baby-blue eyes slowly lumbered to his feet. His gaze locked with the doctor's. The officer wiped his eyes, struggling to get the words out.

"I just need to know, Doc. Can you give me an honest answer? Is he going to make it? I just want the truth."

The doctor looked up at this man-mountain, and his heart broke. He struggled to keep it together then cleared his throat. "I cannot give you a positive yes. I wish I could, but I cannot see beyond right now. But I hope with all my heart that he makes it. We have done all that we can, now the rest is up to God."

He turned and hurriedly left the room before they could see the tears getting ready to flow down his cheeks.

48

The second ambulance carrying Liam and his dad quickly followed behind the first. Bringing up the rear was a third ambulance containing Seth and Steve. Their father, David, had regained consciousness but was having a great deal of difficulty breathing. The pain was so excruciating all he could do was moan continuously as he lay on the gurney, his head elevated, and an oxygen mask over his nose and mouth.

He was whisked off to the radiology department where x-rays showed that he was bleeding from his lung, which was punctured from the broken ribs. His wife, Brenda, was present when he arrived, and her heart tore into tiny pieces as she watched her entire family crying in pain and unable to help them.

"Who would do something like this?" she cried. She looked on helplessly, torn between following the stretcher that was taking her husband to the Operating Room or staying beside Liam, her helpless, unresponsive baby boy.

She chose to stay with her son, and what mother wouldn't? He remained unconsciousness, and so in her state of anguish she continued to hover over him as only a mother can. Silently she prayed that he would sense her presence and open his eyes, if only for a moment. She comforted herself by gently stroking his hair and moaning sweet motherly things in his ears. He had been rushed to the radiology department as soon as he had entered the ER, and the doctors were anxiously awaiting his x-ray results.

Finally, the doctor emerged from the radiology department and walked over to Mrs. Whelan. She looked anxiously at him as he approached and introduced himself.

"Let's go somewhere where we can talk in private," he said to her. Together they walked to a small room located off the main ER. As they walked, he gently guided her by the elbow. He pushed open the door, they entered, and she sat quietly in one of the many vacant chairs.

"What do the x-rays show, Doctor?" asked Mrs. Whelan anxiously.

"It's inconclusive, so we'll need to do some additional tests. Because he sustained a blow to the head, we need to do what is called a brain imaging, or a CT scan. This will help determine the severity of the injury and show how much bleeding or swelling there is in his skull."

She nodded as she heard the news, thankful that it was not worse but hoping it could have been better. "Why is he still asleep, Doctor," she asked nervously.

"He has what is called a concussion," said the doctor. "This is a head injury that results in a temporary loss of brain function, which affects how the brain works for a while."

"Do you know when he will wake up?" she asked.

"No I don't, and no one can predict that with any degree of certainty. However, we will admit him to the Pediatric ICU and keep him there for observation. Don't worry, he'll receive the best care we can give." He touched her shoulders sympathetically and watched as she fought to control her tears.

"Thank you, Doctor. My husband just went to the operating room, and I don't know how long he will be there. What about my other son and our helper? They were hurt as well," she asked worriedly.

"I'm not taking care of them, but I'll ask their doctor to come over and talk with you, and I'll talk with you later. Bye, Mrs. Whelan." He shook her hands, turned, and left the room.

Seth and Steve were given some strong pain medicine before they were taken to radiology. Youth was on their side, and so they were in much better condition than the others. Both had sustained fractured ribs along with some bruising, but no internal organs were damaged. As they made their way from the radiology department, Mrs. Whelan ran to hug them both, tears running unashamedly down her face. Seth winced at the pain in his side from his mom hugging him so hard, but he held it in like a man.

Holding his cheeks with both hands, she looked into her son's eyes as only a mother can.

"How are you feeling?" she asked.

"Not bad, Mom," Seth replied.

Turning to Steve, she asked the same question. "And you Steve?"

"Not bad, Mrs. Whelan, just a bit sore," Steve replied.

"How's Dad?" asked Seth.

"He's in the operating room since…" she looked at her watch. "Oh, I can't believe it's so late. It's hard to believe that this all happened in just one day." She shook her head as if to clear it before continuing. "Anyway, your dad has been in the operating room for two hours now. He should be out pretty soon. I hope everything went okay," she said worriedly.

Looking at his mom, her eyes red from crying, Seth's heart bled for her. He hugged her again to reassure her. "Everything will be fine, Mom. Don't worry." The three moved together as one, looking for a quiet place to patiently await the news about the rest of the family.

Seth and Steve were being discharged home as their injuries were not life-threatening. Before discharge from the ER, it was a requirement that all patients receive a written set of discharge instructions. As they waited, they observed a nurse with some papers heading in their direction. She was an attractive blonde with blue-grey eyes that looked like she belonged on the pages of a fashion magazine instead of in a noisy ER. As she headed toward them, both young men looked at each other and smiled. Considering everything that had transpired so far, it seemed that luck was about to smile on them, and this was about to be the best part of their entire day. It was not rocket science, and no, it did not require much thinking to imagine the thoughts that were running through the minds of these two young men.

"Follow me, gentlemen." She smiled and beckoned for them to follow her. They entered a small room nearby. From that point on, they were putty in her hands, and they would follow her to the ends of the earth if she asked. Closing the door to block out the tumult of the ER, they could finally hear themselves speak. As soon as they were seated, the nurse handed them two pages of typed instructions.

"Okay, fellows. My name is Julia, and these are your discharge instructions. I'm going to review them with you both, and you're expected to follow these instructions when you get home. Let me know if you have questions or if I'm going too fast," she began.

"As the doctor told you, you both have sustained fractured ribs, but this is not life-threatening. The healing process usually takes at least four to six weeks. During this time, you will be feeling a lot of pain. Don't wait until the pain gets so severe that you're unable to breathe normally." She handed them both a prescription.

"This is a prescription for pain pills. You can have it filled at our pharmacy downstairs if you so choose, or at your local pharmacy. As soon as you feel pain, take a pill as prescribed, but no more than every four hours. If you wait too long, then the medicine will take a longer time to be effective. Don't try to be macho about this." She looked at them and smiled, hoping they had heard and understood her instructions and not just thinking about the way she looked. She had seen that goofy look on the faces of so many men before, and not just on the faces of patients. They smiled back.

Returning to the instructions, she continued. "You can place some ice on the area to help reduce the swelling. It really helps. Get plenty of rest, and take some deep breaths and cough at least once every hour even if you don't feel the need. Coughing will help prevent the onset of pneumonia and also prevent your lungs from collapsing." She held onto her sides to demonstrate how to make coughing less painful.

"Are there any questions?" she asked.

"No," they replied in unison.

"Okay. If you think of any questions, or if you have any problems breathing or you start running a high fever, please call us." She pointed to the phone number written on the instruction sheet.

They nodded yes.

"I will need your signatures here and here." She pointed to the spaces on the forms. "Your signature indicates that the instructions were explained to you and that you understood them."

They both affixed their signatures to the spaces indicated, and Nurse Julia collected the original copies, leaving them with the carbon copies. Before making her exit to the chaos that was the ER, she paused, allowing the men one long last look before their angel of mercy departed. She smiled as she headed for the door. "Good luck, fellows, take care of yourselves," she said.

Their hearts fluttered in their chests, causing a small twinge of pain at the site of their injury. But who cared? That smile was worth it all.

"Thank you," they replied, and then she was gone.

49

Officer Harvey had been in excellent health, a physically strong man, and he continued to fight a brave fight day after day.

It was now the fourth day since he had been injured, and during this time, his family never left his side. Not his wife and grown children, not his sisters or his grandchildren, and most of all, not his fraternity police brothers. Not knowing what he was capable of hearing or understanding, they constantly offered words of encouragement.

"You can do it, Michael," his wife, Colleen, whispered in his ears. "We're planning a big party for your new grandson, Sam, but we're all waiting until you get home."

"Grandpa, I got a new fire truck. I need you to teach me how to drive it," three-year-old Toby told him. "Wake up, Grandpa. I want to play with my fire truck."

"Mike, there's a little league forming, and by unanimous decision, you have been voted to be head coach. Practice starts soon, and we're depending on you, so hurry and wake up, brother," said his patrol partner.

"Dad, Bob finally popped the question. I'm engaged. I'm waiting for you to walk me down the aisle," said Marlene, his middle daughter.

Despite all the positive messages, Michael made no response. Tears were shed openly and in private. Prayers were said and candles lit, all hoping he would return to them. Live flowers were not allowed in the ICU, but they were constantly being delivered. The family would read the cards aloud and tell Michael who sent them. The flowers were then donated to other units, also to the hospital chapel, while others were taken home by family members. The walls in his room were covered with get-well cards of all shapes and sizes, everyone wishing him a speedy recovery. His wife, Colleen, would read the cards to him out loud, all the while praying he would at least show some sign that he heard.

"Mike, I'll save the cards for you to read when you wake up," she told him. He gave no sign that he heard.

Late in the evening, he moaned, and his eyes flickered open. Everyone's spirit lifted as they crowded around his bed, positive he was about to wake up. Doctor Martin was summoned. He did a thorough examination, including a neurological exam, but no obvious change was noted.

"He's doing better, isn't he, Doctor? He's waking up, right?" his wife asked, smiling hopefully at Dr. Martin.

The doctor gave a smile and responded. "Mrs. Harvey, it's a very good sign. We just have to wait and see. Sometimes patients may be awake and alert for only a few minutes the first day but gradually stay awake for longer and longer periods."

Throughout the night, Michael continued moaning, his eyes roving around as if trying to determine where he was. Thinking he might be in pain, the doctor instructed the nurses to increase his pain medication. As morning approached, his blood pressure started to fall, as did his heart rate. The nurses increased the vasopressor medication used to constrict the blood vessels and raise the blood pressure. This worked for a short while, but his vitals were not sustainable, and soon the process had to be repeated again.

On the sixth day, the doctor called a family conference. As the time approached, a steady stream of family members headed toward the conference room located at the end of the ICU. The room was of reasonable size and consisted of a long conference table at the center surrounded by the usual conference room chairs. The chairs were all occupied, and there was barely standing room as family members and members of the police brotherhood crowded in. The room was quiet with a soft undercurrent of tension running through. Everyone appeared to be in deep thought, all wondering about the news that was to be delivered.

Dead silence enveloped the room as Dr. Martin entered followed by two of his colleagues. They squeezed their way into the room and made it to the head of the table. The door closed softly behind them. Thirty pairs of eyes zoomed in on the doctor's face, as if trying to read his mind. The intensity on their faces spurred the doctor and his team to deliver the news as quickly and as painlessly as possible. Dr. Martin started the meeting by recognizing his colleagues.

"As promised, we're here to give you an update on Officer Harvey's condition. Let me start by introducing Dr. Ivan McDonald, cardiologist, and Dr. James Henry, our pulmonologist. Together we have worked diligently toward bringing Officer Harvey through this horrific ordeal. I know that you have all been hopeful throughout this entire process, so I thought it was time to update you on his condition."

He hesitated as he turned to face his colleague. "First, I would like Dr. McDonald to explain his role in Officer Harvey's case." He stepped aside, making room for Dr. McDonald.

Dr. McDonald looked at the sea of faces, breathed deeply, and then started. "Officer Harvey is a very strong man, and he's fighting with all that he's got. Let me assure you, we're also fighting as hard as we can to bring him through this. I'm a cardiologist, and my main focus is on the heart and how it functions. If there are any questions that you would…" He didn't complete the sentence as Mrs. Harvey raised her hand. Dr. McDonald recognized her.

"Yes, Mrs. Harvey?"

"Doctor, can you tell me why his heart rate is so irregular? One minute it's up, and next it's down."

"That's a very good question. Well, your heart rate or pulse determines the strength of your heart. It's an indication of how hard our heart is working. The heart rate tend to accelerate when the body is stressed, either by bacterial or viral infections, and especially when it's accompanied by fever. Your husband has been fighting off several infections for which he is receiving antibiotics. As soon as these infections clear up, his heart rate will eventually return to normal."

Another hand went up and was quickly recognized. "Do you think he's going to make it, Doctor? It's been six days, and he's still not waking up."

"These things take time, and as I said, he's putting up a good fight. I don't have a straightforward yes or no as to when he will wake up, but we're doing everything we can."

On and on the questions kept coming.

"When will he be able to speak?" one officer asked.

"When will the breathing tube be removed?" his daughter asked.

"What's causing the fever?" his son asked.

All questions were answered to everyone's satisfaction, and finally, Doctor Martin intervened and introduced his other colleague.

"Dr. Henry, our pulmonologist, specializes in the area of the lungs. He's prepared to take your questions." Before the doctor had a chance to introduce himself, the questions started flowing.

"When will he be able to breathe on his own, Doctor?" asked one of his sons.

"Does he have pneumonia?" his daughter asked.

"Can he hear us when we're talking to him?" one officer asked.

Dr. Henry patiently received and answered each question to the satisfaction of everyone. Soon no more questions were forthcoming, so Dr. Martin thanked everyone and told them he would keep them informed as needed.

50

Members of the police force were up in arms. Not only the local officers but others from the adjoining states had joined in. One of their own had been attacked. It was an unspoken decision that no stone would be left unturned in an effort to locate this perpetrator. There was no place he could hide that they would not find him.

No sooner had they realized the enormity of the crime than an all-points bulletin had been issued. Based on the description given by Seth and Steven, a police artist had sketched almost an exact likeness of Luke Foster. This was currently being circulated throughout the county and the state. The local television stations were broadcasting his image every fifteen minutes, and the radio stations were announcing all the available information they could get their hands on. Of course, Luke heard all this on his car radio and knew he was going to be in for a tough time. He was no fool. He knew he was in deep trouble, and right now, his only savior was staying on this seldom traveled road on which he was driving.

For the past few days, he had stayed hidden until well after dark, not emerging until it was well past midnight. As was his new practice, when he emerged from his hiding place, the first order of business was to find a farm or some other dwelling from which he could get some food. For days now, he had been thinking of ditching his current mode of transport. He refused to leave anything up to chance.

"I'm sure everyone will be on the lookout for a red mustang," he said to himself. "I need something less conspicuous."

He had been driving for over an hour and had not spotted another car. But then, it was a little after midnight, and this was farm country where people went to bed when the sun went down. The houses were few and far apart, and he was on the verge of giving up when he spotted a building that resembled a farmhouse. All the lights were off except for one lonely low-watt outdoor bulb. This suited him just fine as his intentions were less than pristine. The large wooden gates leading to the farm were closed, but on closer inspection, he found they were unlocked. As carefully as he could, he opened them all the way and quietly glided into the property.

As he neared the building, his inner voice told him to kill the engine, which he did. The worst that could possibly happen was to be discovered before even starting the job he had come to do. He quietly coasted toward the back of a barn-like structure and then stashed the mustang out of sight among some tall grass. He was in no hurry to get caught tonight! He circled around the car, making sure that no part of it was exposed.

"Better to be safe than sorry," he told himself.

It was quiet and pitch black outdoors. The moon seemed to have taken the night off, and not even the crickets were chirping. He turned the car radio off then sat quietly and listened, every sense in his body on high alert. No sounds came from inside the house. Even the dogs appeared to be sleeping. After his eyes had adjusted to the darkness, he decided he would wait another five minutes before making his move. He looked at his watch one more time.

"At least my watch still works," he said to himself. "If things continue this way, I'll have to sell it for whatever I can get. This money is not going to last forever."

The night was chilly, so Luke wrapped his arms around himself to generate some heat. He had still not bought a warm coat, but he knew he would have to do so before long. Without making a sound, he opened the car door and slowly stepped out. Darkness enveloped him like a cloak as he stealthily made his way to the building that appeared to be the main house. The night remained still, and the grass under his feet felt as smooth as velvet. It seemed as though a steamroller had just rolled over it, removing all imperfections. Approaching a back door, he quietly turned the knob. It was unlocked.

Luke smiled to himself. *This is so easy*, he thought. *Why do people who live in the country think it's so safe? They keep refusing to lock their doors!*

Bringing his attention back to the business at hand, he continued turning the knob. The lock gave a squeak. It was a tiny squeak, but in the dead of night it sounded almost like a bomb going off. Luke held his breath, waiting for some response from inside the house.

Nothing!

"This is not what I came for," he said to himself. "But I need some energy before I can do anything else."

Holding the knob firmly in place, he waited a while before he continued turning. He gently pushed the door until finally, with just enough room to allow himself to enter, he squeezed himself through and stepped into what appeared to be the kitchen. He could smell the chicken that the family must have had for dinner.

Oh, what I wouldn't give for a piece of that chicken, he thought.

It did not take long for his eyes to adjust to the darkness. He soon located the refrigerator, and his feet made a beeline in that direction. It was as if that fridge was calling his name. His stomach rumbled in anticipation, and his mouth started salivating at the thought of tasting some good homemade food.

How long had it been since he had eaten a good home-cooked meal? Seemed like a lifetime ago. He had not taken more than five steps in the direction of the fridge when the sound of a rifle being cocked reached his ear. His legs stopped in midstride as his right hand slowly reached behind him to remove the weapon he had confiscated from the injured officer.

Too late! It was not there. He had left it in the car. Of all the dumb luck!

He peered into the darkness and noticed what appeared to be stairs leading to an upper floor. He had not seen it when he had first entered the house, but he could see the outline of what appeared to be someone pointing a rifle in his direction. Now was definitely not the time to confirm whether it was male or female. His instincts told him to run for his life, and putting thought into action, he quickly turned and sprinted toward the door.

"Stop!" came a shout from behind, but Luke was in no mood to take orders tonight. He picked up speed and quickly made it to the door. He grabbed hold of the knob and was on the verge of squeezing his body through the doorway, but the space was proving to be too small. Two rapid-fire blasts erupted from the stairs, one after the other. In the stillness of the night and to Luke's ears, they sounded like a million firecrackers exploding on the Fourth of July.

Suddenly his right leg felt as if it were on fire. He screamed as he crumbled to the floor, his entire body drowning in a sea of pain.

51

The 911 call came into the police precinct at one thirty in the morning. "This is Joseph Sullivan at the Sullivan farm on Route 20," he calmly told the operator. "I just shot a young fellow in my kitchen. He's still breathing, but you need to send an ambulance. He's losing quite a bit of blood and messing up the tile on my kitchen floor."

"Where did you shoot him, sir?" asked the operator.

"In the leg," the farmer drawled.

"Okay, Mr. Sullivan. The police and ambulance are on their way," replied the operator.

Soon the Sullivan farm was awash with a sea of activity. The flashing blue lights from the police cruisers mixed with the red lights from the ambulances and fire trucks lit up the night sky like a country fair. The chatter from their police radios and scanners quickly reached a crescendo. No sooner had the police taken a look at Luke than they knew who he was. However, they were not going to play a guessing game tonight, so a description was quickly relayed to the various precincts. Then the waiting game began.

The officers congregated in small groups talking among themselves while waiting to receive word on the true identification of their prisoner. They were loaded down with their Kevlar vests, pockets bulging with the standard equipment that all police officers are required to carry.

It did not take long for Luke's identity to be verified, and from the looks on their faces, they all knew that the search for the shooter of their police brother had come to an end.

One look on their faces, and Luke knew that they knew exactly who he was. *They won't be treating me with kid gloves tonight*, he thought.

The EMTs lifted him onto a gurney. His wounds were attended to, the blood flow stanched; all the time he screamed and writhed in pain. "Can I have something for pain, please?" he begged, tears rolling down his face. A group of officers headed over toward him, determination written on their faces.

"Are you Luke Foster?" asked one officer. Despite the pain he was feeling, his brain had not been affected, and he was determined to use it to its fullest. So he took his time responding, which did nothing to improve the officer's temperament. There was really no way out of this situation, and Luke realized it, so he finally responded, "Yes, I am."

The officer reached for his well-worn notebook, flipped a few pages, and started reading. "You have the right to remain silent. Anything you say, can and will be used against you…" With that, the handcuffs were unceremoniously attached to his wrist. The finality of the cuffs clicking in place brought Luke to the realization that he was no longer a free man.

He was loaded into the ambulance and whisked away to the emergency room. As the caravan of police cruisers followed behind the ambulance, Luke knew that from that time forward, freedom as he knew it was no longer his to take for granted. But then, you just never know!

It was now three weeks since that fateful night at the Sullivan farm when Luke was arrested. Luckily the gunshot wounds he had sustained were not very serious. No bones were broken, and no major organs or blood vessels were compromised. He had spent only two weeks in the hospital and the remainder of the time in the local jail. He commuted to the hospital for daily physical therapy and was now able to move about quite well with the aid of a cane. He was never out of sight of a police officer, and he knew this was pretty much how his life was going to be from here on out. This was an extremely difficult pill for him to swallow, and he was finding it more difficult as each day approached.

He was classified as a dangerous felon; after all, he had attacked an officer. This act alone held him in disdain, even among other prisoners. Privileges that the other detainees enjoyed were severely restricted for him. Some of his basic rights could not be deprived, but still he did not come by them easily.

Finally the date of his trial arrived, and this was one trip to which he was not looking forward. He had been assigned a court-appointed attorney whom he had met with on a regular basis. The fateful trip started out from the jail at nine o'clock sharp. The route to the court house was the same as he had traveled daily to his physiotherapy sessions. The therapy center was about two miles from the jail and the courthouse an additional three miles. Luke's mind had always gone into overdrive whenever he passed by a stretch of deserted road. It was bordered by tall trees and thick foliage. He always enjoyed the solitary view. After all, who knew when an opportunity might present itself for him to use more than just the view?

As a general rule, two officers would accompany each prisoner to their hearing. However, the other assigned officer had encountered an emergency that morning that prevented him from making the trip, and a replacement was not readily available. Luke was aware of this rule, but who knew; maybe he could use this situation to his advantage. As the van approached the long deserted strip of road, the transport vehicle suddenly started making unusual sounds. Smoke started spurting from the engine and into the cab. Both driver and prisoner started coughing, and before long, they were finding it difficult to catch a breath. The driver coasted to a stop, opened the front windows, and turned on the exhaust fan. After making sure the prisoner was secure, he exited the van. He opened the hood and looked at the engine to see if he could identify the source of the problem.

This was Luke's opportunity, and never one to look a gift horse in the mouth, he was not going to let this slip by.

"This might be my only chance," he said to himself. Using the handcuffs, he started banging on the window to attract the driver's attention.

"What's your problem?" the driver yelled.

Luke yelled back, but neither one was able to understand what the other was saying. Already frustrated from being unable to find the cause of the problem, the driver angrily yanked open the door.

"What do you want?" he yelled angrily.

Luke grabbed on to his stomach, his face contorted in pain. "I need to use the toilet. I must have eaten some bad food this morning, but I need to go, or else there's going to be an accident." The driver scratched his head, trying to decide what he should do. Luke continued moaning.

"Just hold on," replied the driver. "Maybe it'll pass. I had the same thing for breakfast, and I'm fine."

"Well, everyone's different!" yelled Luke. "Please, let me go. You can watch me. I won't do anything, I promise."

The driver finally relented and helped him out of the van. "Don't try anything funny," he warned. Luke presented his wrists for the cuffs to be removed. The driver shook his head. "No, I can't do that. You'll just have to manage."

Luke gave him a look of frustration. "Have you ever tried going to the restroom with your hands cuffed?" he asked.

The driver wavered for a minute. "Okay, I guess I'm a softie. Don't make me regret this." Luke shook his head. "No you won't. I promise."

The driver unlocked the cuffs. No sooner had the lock clicked and Luke had one arm free than he coldcocked the driver to the side of his head. The driver stumbled backward, dazed. With arms flailing, he tried steadying himself but failed. As he hit the ground, Luke reached for the bunch of keys. He thought about taking the officer's gun but decided against it. He quickly released his other arm then his legs. He threw the keys into the bushes and took off running.

"I knew these woods would serve me well one day," he mumbled as he headed deeper into the woods.

52

The practical nursing program is the quickest route to becoming a nurse, and Margaret decided that she would follow this path. She completed all the required science and non-science courses in addition to the clinical hands-on practice. Her happiness knew no bounds when she had been accepted into the LPN program. She promised herself not to let anything or anyone divert her from her goal. Before she knew it, a year had quickly gone by. She had completed the program and was now in the process of studying and hopefully passing the National Council Licensure Examination in order to become licensed.

Life was not easy for Margaret as she held on to her job at the Blue Bird diner and carried a full complement of credits. Luckily, her boss, Lou, was extremely flexible and had juggled the schedule to accommodate her. She knew she would have a hard time saying good-bye to him and her coworkers at the diner, and with a bit of luck, that time was fast approaching.

Today was her day off, and she was expecting two of her classmates to do some serious studying in preparation for the upcoming exam. She drained the last drop of coffee from her cup and gathered all the books she needed. She took her seat at the kitchen table and, as if on cue, her doorbell rang. As she headed for the front door, the doorbell rang again.

"Patience, Barb. I'm coming," she called out.

Margaret never failed to look through the peephole before opening her door, and today was no different. As she looked through the peephole, she could see Barbara with her hands cupped beside her face, leaning forward while trying to peer through the small glass insert located at either side of the main door.

As Margaret opened the door, Barbara, her flamboyant African American friend, entered and threw her arms around her, hugging her hard.

"Hey, girl. What took you so long to open the door?"

Margaret struggled to release herself from Barbara's suffocating grip and wrinkled her nose as an overpowering smell assaulted her nostrils. "What are you wearing, Barb? Whatever it is, it smells like you took a bath in it."

Barb let go of Margaret and pouted, pretending her feelings were hurt. Anyone who knew Barb well knew that was her way of attracting attention to herself, so Margaret chose to ignore her.

"Girl, can't you recognize expensive perfume when you smell it?" Barb asked, giving Margaret one of her "you've hurt my feelings" look.

Margaret returned her own "I'm sorry if your feelings are hurt, but I really meant it" look in return. While all this drama was taking place, their other friend, Katy, the quiet one of the group, managed to squeeze her way into the condo and quietly closed the door. Margaret turned away from Barb and welcomed her.

"Hi, Katy. Ready for a hard day of hitting the books?" asked Margaret, smiling.

"That's why I'm here," replied Katy, taking a seat at the table.

Katy was a beautiful, diminutive blonde with hazel eyes and a quiet disposition. Though quiet, she was wise in so many ways. She was always the voice of reason and the most serious and business-minded of the group. So taking a cue from her, both Barb and Margaret took their seats and settled in for a few hours of serious studying.

53

Luke headed deeper and deeper into the woods as fast as his legs would take him. This was no easy feat as the branches and thick foliage fought to hold him back. He knew that before long, the entire state police force with their K9 tracking dogs would be hot on his tracks. Although it was daylight, the sunlight was barely able to penetrate the thick foliage and reach the woodland floor. In addition, this was all new terrain, and Luke had no idea where he was headed. However, turning back was not an option, and so he kept going.

For his court appearance, he was dressed in a blue shirt and dark pants, so he was not easily visible neither from land or air. As he plowed into the darkness of the woods, he thought to himself, *Thank God I'm not wearing the usual orange jumpsuit. I'd be such an easy target.*

Deeper and deeper he continued into the woods. For a while he could see nothing but bushes and darkness before him. He swatted at flies and other insects that wanted to make a meal of him. His long-sleeved shirt spared him from being eaten alive by the mosquitoes that kept up a constant buzz. However, the thorns and bushes were less than kind as they continued grabbing at him with every step he took. He could hear dogs barking in the distance and hoped against hope that they were not already on his tracks.

Somewhere during his flight, his watch got snagged by a sturdy vine. He tried his best to retrieve it, but the vine proved to be the stronger opponent, so he had no choice but to leave it behind. After a while, barely able to catch his breath, he leaned against an old tree trunk. He knew this was not the time to rest, but his lungs were crying out, and he needed to heed the call. Soon he dragged himself up and continued on his way, still not sure where he was headed.

The sun barely penetrated to the ground below, and this made the leaves wet and very slippery. Carefully maneuvering his way around a large rock, he lost his balance, slipped, and landed hard on his butt. The slippery mess of rotting leaves on the forest floor made it easy for him to keep sliding. After uttering a few choice words, he managed to regain his balance. He stood and tried brushing off the mess as best he could then continued on his way. He had no sense of how much ground he had covered, or what time it was, as he had no watch to consult. All he knew was that his clothes were a mess; he was hungry, thirsty, extremely tired, and in a very foul mood.

The bushes finally started thinning out, and Luke started catching brief glimpses of an occasional house in the distance. Finally, he spotted a clearing a short distance ahead and headed in that direction. As he drew closer, he could hear the sound of an occasional vehicle.

"Thank God, finally, a road," he sighed.

He cautiously approached the edge of the woods and looked in both directions. No cars or people were visible. Taking a good look at his clothes, he realized that no one would offer him a ride in his present condition. He looked worse than a bum!

He searched his pockets and found a small hair comb. He breathed a sigh of relief. "I'm glad you didn't get lost," he said, looking at the small hair comb that had been miraculously spared. There was nothing he could do about his clothing, but at least he could do something with his hair. With no time to spare, he brushed himself off one more time, climbed the stone barrier, and started walking, all the time hoping a Good Samaritan would come by and offer him a ride.

Soon the sound of an approaching vehicle reached his ears. He stopped and looked in the direction of the vehicle, unsure if this was friend or foe. A beat-up farm van pulled up alongside him, and an old farmer called out to him through the open window.

"Hi, young fellow. Look like you could use a ride. Where are you headed?"

Luke thought quickly, remembering what he had told the first officer in Chastain. *Better to stick to the same plan*, he thought to himself.

"I'm heading for Hartford. My friends dropped me off down the road, so I'm looking for a ride. How far is Hartford from here?"

The old farmer removed his hat and scratched his head as he pondered the question. "About eight or ten miles, give or take a mile," he replied. "Hop in. I'll take you as far as I can."

The farmer looked him over and smiled. "What happened to your clothes? Looks like you were in a fight."

"Not exactly," replied Luke. "I was a bit careless. I didn't look where I was going and fell into a puddle."

The old farmer looked him over once more. "You forgot your coat? It's getting quite nippy."

Luke did not reply. He walked around the side and climbed into the van and sat next to the farmer. He tried making himself as comfortable as possible, but as careful as he had been, the bugs had done a job on his exposed skin. He tried not to scratch, but it was unavoidable, and soon the old farmer couldn't help but ask. "The bugs got you, son?"

"Yes," Luke replied and kept on scratching.

"It's been raining quite a bit around here lately. Those critters can be pretty mean. Just spray it with some mosquito spray. It'll be better quicker than you know."

"Thanks," Luke replied. Soon they came to a fork in the road, and the farmer stopped.

"This is as far as I go." He pointed his gnarled fingers to the left. "Just follow that road for a bit, and you should soon see the sign leading to the highway before long. You should be able to hitch a ride without much problem."

Luke opened the door, hopped out, and slammed the door. "Thanks for the ride sir."

"You're welcome, young man. Good luck," the farmer replied.

Luke hesitated before moving on. His stomach was making funny noises, which heralded hunger. Finally, hunger won out. He put aside his pride and asked, "Do you have anything to eat? I'm kind of hungry, and I'm not sure when I'll get to a restaurant." The farmer reached into his lunchbox and pulled out a wrapped package along with a bottle of water. He handed it to Luke.

"Today's your lucky day. My wife made this for my lunch, but I was too busy to eat. It's all yours."

Luke accepted it gratefully and headed on his way. "Yes, indeed," he said to himself. "You don't know how right you are, old man. Today is really my lucky day."

54

Officer Harvey's condition continued to improve at a roller coaster pace. One day he was awake and alert, the next day he was not. The breathing tube had been removed, and he was now breathing on his own without difficulty.

"I'm so happy…to get rid of that tube," he said to the doctor in between breaths.

"I'm happy that you're happy," said the doctor, smiling. "Next will be the chest tube, then you can start walking around. Before you know it, you'll be running a marathon."

"We'll run it together, Doc," the officer replied, smiling for the first time.

Within a few days, his lungs had inflated substantially, and the chest tube drainage had decreased in volume, color, and consistency. After multiple chest x-rays, the chest tube was removed. The wound appeared to be free from infection, so a sterile Vaseline gauze dressing was applied followed by a dry dressing. He reluctantly began his deep-breathing exercises to help his lung heal and stay inflated. The only area of difficulty was his ability to stay out of bed.

"You need to sit up for longer periods," his wife told him.

"I get too tired," he would reply as he crawled back into bed. All attempts to get him to ambulate failed miserably. The more encouragement he received from the doctors, nurses, and family, the more adamant he would get about staying out of bed. Even the encouragement from his police brothers failed to raise his spirits. The hours he spent in bed sleeping were now becoming longer than the time he stayed out.

"I'm worried," his wife said to Dr. Edwards, the chief of the ICU. "He seems to be depressed. He was always such a fun-loving person. I'm not sure what to do."

"I'll get the psychologist to take a look at him. I hope he'll open up and talk. Maybe something is bothering him. He's been through a lot, and sometimes it takes a while for the mind to adjust to the trauma that the body has suffered," continued Dr. Edwards.

"Thanks, Doc. I sure hope that works," replied Mrs. Harvey.

It was the day of his appointment with the psychologist, and Officer Harvey did not seem to care one way or the other. At 6:00 a.m. he started running a low-grade fever of 100.2 degrees Fahrenheit. At first there was no immediate cause for concern. He refused his breakfast, telling the nurse, "Just leave it on the table, nurse."

"Officer, it's going to get cold. Why not have it now?" the nurse encouraged.

"It won't get cold, I'll be up soon," he assured her.

Half an hour passed, and the nurse returned only to find his meal remained untouched. "Officer Harvey, you didn't have your breakfast. How are you going to get your strength back if you refuse to eat?"

"I have no appetite now. I promise I'll do better for lunch," he said to the nurse.

The nurse kept a close eye on him as did Brian, the Physician assistant. His vital signs were stable, but for some reason, something just seemed a bit off. The nurse elevated the head of the bed. "Michael, turn on your side, please," she told him.

Michael opened his eyes and attempted to sit up. He was seized with a sudden bout of coughing, causing him to fight for each breath. As one bout of coughing subsided, he struggled for the next breath. The coughing was now accompanied by spurting of bright-red blood, the amount increasing with each coughing episode. "My…chest…hurts," he gasped, grabbing onto his chest and struggling to catch another breath. The nurse pushed the emergency bell, and Brian the PA came running. One quick look told him the officer was in big trouble. *If I don't move fast, I'll have one dead patient on my hands*, he thought to himself.

"Michael, take slow, deep breaths," Brian coaxed, but the patient was in far too much discomfort to comply. Brian looked at the cardiac monitor, checked his heart rate, listened to his lungs, and did a quick assessment. "Call radiology stat. We need a chest x-ray, and let's do an EKG," he told the nurse.

As each minute went by, Michael appeared to be in more acute distress. The monitor showed a rapid heart rate with beats at one hundred beats per minute and climbing. Minute by minute he was becoming more exhausted from the constant coughing. Brian knew that his body would not be able to tolerate this onslaught for much longer. Finally, the coughing gradually subsided, and he started breathing normally. Brian breathed a sigh of relief.

"Michael, how are you feeling?" Brian asked.

"A bit better," Michael replied, taking a deep breath. Suddenly the cardiac monitor sounded the emergency alarm. Brian and the nurse both looked up at the monitor. It showed a rapid, erratic heart rate pattern and a very low blood pressure reading. Brian was just in time to see Michael's head loll to the side and his eyes roll backward in his head.

"V-fib," Brian called out.

Wasting no time, he yelled, "Code 8, room 12!" The nurse quickly lowered the head of the bed and opened the patient's gown so his chest was exposed. Adhesive gel electrode pads were applied to his chest, and Brian quickly administered an electric shock.

In the blink of an eye, the room was flooded with doctors, nurses, respiratory therapists, and other essential personnel. Michael was quickly intubated, and the respiratory therapist kept up a steady pace of ambuing. The emergency crash cart was opened and supplies handed out wherever it was needed. As one person tired from administering CPR, a new person took their place. On and on it went, stopping occasionally to check for a palpable pulse or a spontaneous respiration. So far, the only tracings displayed on the monitor were the results of the manual compressions, and the only breaths were those delivered by the ambu bag. Multiple cardioversions and IV emergency medications were showing no results.

Twenty minutes came and went since the initiation of CPR, and the monitor was now showing asystole, but still they labored on. Used needles, catheters, IV bags, and instrument wrappers were scattered around the room, all evidence of the massive effort that was in progress trying to save a life. It was now thirty minutes since CPR was initiated, and exhaustion and frustration was quite evident on the faces of all participants.

The resident turned to Dr. Edwards and asked, "Should we call it?"

"How long has it been?" asked Dr. Edwards.

"Thirty minutes since we started," replied Brian.

"Let's call it," replied Dr. Edwards sadly.

"Time of death, 1:30 p.m." said Brian.

The resident ended his compressions, removed his gloves, and tossed them in the garbage. All that was left now was to deliver the news to Michael's family and friends that he was no longer alive.

55

Margaret and her friends hit the books with a passion, and by noon they had covered just about half of what they had planned on studying. Barbara was the first to call a halt. She got out of her chair, stretched, and yawned.

"It's lunch time. Is there a pizza shop nearby?" she asked, looking at Margaret.

"Not to worry" Margaret smiled, reaching for her cell phone. "I placed an order before you guys came. So I'll just make a quick call for them to deliver it."

The delivery was made, and soon they were delving into pizza, salad, garlic knots, and sodas. They thoroughly enjoyed the delicious fare, and soon the two pizza boxes were almost empty. The garlic knots were gone and the two-liter bottle of soda drained. Only a portion of the salad remained.

Suddenly Katy started loosening the button of her jeans while holding onto her stomach. "I can't eat another bite," she moaned.

"Same here," returned Margaret. "How about you, Barb?" asked Katy.

"I'm just about ready to pass out, but I need to finish this last garlic knot. It's so good." She kept on licking her fingers, savoring the last drop of oil, determined that nothing go to waste.

"I'm ready for a nap," Katy said, moving slowly from the kitchen table to the couch in the living room. That was quickly followed up with, "Me too," by both Margaret and Barb. It wasn't long before the only sounds emanating from the condo were the soft breathing of three very sated friends.

There's nothing like a good nap following a great meal. This was the thought on the minds of the three friends after waking up two hours later. Katy was the first to wake up from their siesta. She shook the others awake.

"Hey, guys. Are we going to do some more studying? It's two o'clock," she called out, looking at her watch. "There's still time to get some more work done."

"Oh, do we really have to?" asked Barb sleepily, turning over and burrowing into the sofa.

Margaret came fully awake. "What time is it?" she asked, looking at Barb.

"It's five after two," replied Katy.

Margaret quickly jumped up all flustered. "Oh my gosh! I never planned to sleep this long. Let's get back to studying. I took the day off to study, so did you guys. Let's get back to it."

One by one they trudged off to the restroom and returned recharged and ready to prepare themselves for their future.

56

Luke trudged on along the deserted road. He was tired but not so much that he did not keep his ears attuned for the sound of any vehicle that would offer him a ride. "I'll take a ride from just about anyone," he said to himself. "Anyone except law enforcement."

It was getting late, and the temperature was starting to drop even further. He had seen neither a car nor another human being since the farmer had dropped him off earlier. He was cold and lonely, and he was a fugitive. How much worse could life get? With his hands deep in his pockets, shoulders hunched forward, trying to give himself some warmth, he was oblivious to the small sports car that pulled up behind him. The driver blared his horn. Frightened beyond belief, Luke's heart rate sped to the upper limits as adrenaline pumped through his body. Should he stay and fight, or should he take flight?

He was about to take off running when the driver called out laughingly. "Sorry, I didn't mean to scare you. You just looked so deep in thought I just had to do something to attract your attention." Luke slowed down, allowing his heart rate to return to normal.

"Can I drop you somewhere? I'm Danny," the driver offered, hand outstretched.

Luke took one look at the driver, decided he was too young to be a threat, so he smiled and replied, "Hi, I'm Luke. I'm heading for Hartford. Are you going anywhere near there?"

"Hop in. This is your lucky day. That's where I'm heading, and I could sure use the company," replied Danny.

In a flash, Luke was settled comfortably in one of the most expensive sports car he had ever had the pleasure of riding in. The seat was leather and felt as soft as butter. The most expensive gadgets were displayed on the dashboard, some of which Luke had never seen before.

"This is really cool," he said, looking around awestruck. "This must cost a fortune."

"Yes, it did, but it's only money," replied Danny, laughing as he gunned the engine. The highway soon came in sight, and in a flash, the car went from zero to sixty. The scenery flew by as Luke got to know his new friend without revealing too much about himself. They continued chatting like old friends while the car ate up the miles and darkness quietly fell. The exit sign for Hartford flashed by, and Luke suddenly realized he had no idea where he would be staying the night.

Seeming to read his thoughts, Danny asked, "So, Luke, where would you like to be dropped off?"

Luke fidgeted for a quick second while trying to formulate a plan.

"The truth is I haven't been here before, so I really don't know the area. But my cousin told me to wait for him at the first diner after the Hartford exit. I guess this is it," Luke smiled. "I hope he'll recognize me," he continued, looking down at his soiled clothing. "But I have no choice, as I told you before, I was mugged, and I lost all my stuff. They took everything, even my wallet. I was never so happy to see anyone as I did when you stopped and offered me a ride. Right now, I'm so hungry I could eat a horse."

Danny took the exit ramp, drove a quarter of a mile, and soon pulled into the *diner's* parking lot. From the outside, it looked so warm and inviting. Luke's stomach started doing flip-flops, a reminder that he had not eaten since the old farmer had given him his sandwich earlier.

"I could use a hot meal myself," Danny replied, turning off the engine.

"Come on. My treat," he said, heading for the entrance. Luke quickly followed.

The diner was not very crowded, so they found two seats at a corner table without any difficulty. Soon a smiling waitress walked over.

"Welcome to the Blue Bird diner. My name is Carol, and I'll be your waitress. Our special tonight is homemade beef stew. I can tell you it's very good," she said with a smile.

"I'll take your word for it," replied Luke, returning the menu.

"And I'll have the same," said Danny.

A few tables down sat a young family of five. The three kids appeared to range in age from five years to a few months. The young parents seemed to be having a difficult time controlling their overactive offsprings. One of the other waitresses was doing her best, helping the parents bring back some semblance of order to the ensuing chaos.

As they waited for their meal, Danny and Luke looked around, taking in the ambiance of the diner. Carol soon returned with two bowls of hot delicious-smelling stew along with two heaping bowls of rice and fresh-from-the-oven rolls dripping with warm butter. Mouths salivating, Luke and Danny immediately delved in. No talking was heard until they were halfway through the meal.

"She was right. This really tastes good," said Luke, smiling with his mouth half full.

"I agree," replied Danny, smiling.

Like the other patrons, Luke's attention was again drawn to the table as the antics of the children made it impossible for the parents to enjoy their meal. The waitress was doing her best to assist the parents, but it was clear that the entire situation was heading south. The waitress moved around the table, helping to collect discarded toys and clean up spilled juice. As she turned, Luke caught sight of her face and froze. His fork stopped halfway to his mouth.

"My God, it's Margaret," he mumbled.

Danny looked up from his meal. "Did you say something?" he asked. Luke gave no reply. His full attention was focused on the waitress. Danny followed Luke's line of vision and then smiled. "I can see what has captured your attention. I must say you have excellent taste in women, Luke."

Luke sat transfixed by what he was seeing. Danny snapped his fingers, startling Luke out of his reverie. "Are you okay?" he asked anxiously.

Luke jumped. "Oh...sorry. I'm okay. I just thought I saw someone from my past, but I could be wrong," he replied absentmindedly. He slowly returned to his meal, but he had lost his appetite. Danny paid for the meals and headed outside to resume his journey. "Thanks for the ride, Danny. I hope my cousin will be here soon," Luke said as they walked to Danny's car.

"Are you sure he's coming?" asked Danny.

"I certainly hope so. At least that's what we agreed on before I lost my phone. Can I borrow your phone? I just want to call and let him know I'm here waiting," he said to Danny.

"Sure," said Danny, handing his phone to Luke. He moved away, allowing Luke his privacy. Luke pretended to dial while holding down the off button, hoping all the while that no incoming call would reveal his duplicity. Finishing his call, he walked over to Danny and returned his phone.

"My cousin's on his way. Thanks for helping me out. I really appreciate everything," Luke said, holding out his hands to shake Danny's.

Danny returned the gesture and headed for his car. He stopped and turned. "How are you for money? Can you use a few dollars?' he asked Luke.

Luke acted surprised at the offer. "You've been so kind to me, I don't know if I can impose on you any further."

Ignoring Luke's protest, Danny removed two fifty-dollar bills from his wallet and handed them to Luke. He jumped in his car and headed out of the parking lot.

I guess there are still Good Samaritans out here, Luke thought. *Sorry, I'm just not one of them.*

57

As soon as Danny's brake lights disappeared, Luke turned and headed back into the diner. He had to make sure it was Margaret. If she wasn't, then okay, at least his curiosity would have been satisfied, but he couldn't just walk away not knowing. After all, it had been almost two years, and he knew that people change over time, but this waitress was a dead ringer for Margaret.

There's a saying that everyone has a twin out there somewhere. Well, if this is Margaret's twin, then I want to know.

He casually sauntered to the men's restroom and hid in one of the stalls. If his luck held out, he would stay there until the rest of the customers left for the night. He hoped the patrons were too busy enjoying their meals to notice that he had not returned from the restroom.

He didn't have long to wait, as the few remaining customers started drifting out of the diner. Now all he had to do was wait a bit longer for the lights to go off. He worked himself closer to the door where he could hear the staff talking.

"I'm glad this day is over, I'm so tired," said Carol, the waitress who had served them earlier.

"Me too," replied Margaret's look-alike. "I have to wake up early to do some studying." She yawned and stretched.

"Why don't you go home, Margaret? I can finish up here," said another waitress.

Luke could not believe his ears. *She called her Margaret. It really is her. This is my lucky night!*

The door leading to the rear of the restaurant was unlocked, so he quietly slipped out, closing the door behind him. He headed for the parking lot. The lot was poorly lit, which suited him just fine. He quickly looked around trying to locate Margaret's blue car that she had driven when she fled Plains. He could not locate it anywhere. "I guess she bought a new car." The thought aroused a deep anger within him, but he told himself he could not afford to lose control at this crucial time. He had to keep his mind clear and sharp in order to bring absolute finality to his plans.

He hid in a darkened corner where he could see but not be seen. He was unsure of his plans, but right now he would just wait, and let things work themselves out. He didn't have long to wait. The door opened, and Margaret came out, heading for a dark-red Honda parked some distance from the single low-watt bulb. She stood fumbling in her purse for the car keys, her back toward him. Suddenly a thought struck him. Not waiting to think it through, he sprang from his hiding place and sprinted to where Margaret was still searching for her keys. In one fell swoop, he grabbed her purse and sprinted off into the darkened portion of the parking lot.

Margaret screamed, but the door to the diner was now closed, so no one heard her screams. She quickly ran back and started banging on the door. The door opened, and she rushed in, frightened and out of breath and barely able to speak.

"Margaret, what happened?" Lou asked.

"I was mugged. He took my pocketbook. All of my personal information is in there," she cried hysterically. They sat her in a chair and tried calming her down while crowding around her.

"Give her some air," said Carol, spreading her arms wide, indicating for everyone to move back.

Lou was angry and fit to be tied. He shouted at the men gathered around. "Go, see if you can find him." Two husky cook staff ran to the parking lot to look around but returned shortly.

"He's gone. There's no one there," they told Lou. Lou and the others were still crowding around Margaret.

"Did you get a look at his face?" asked Lou.

"No," replied Margaret. "It all happened so fast, and it was dark, I didn't see his face."

"We need to call the police," another waitress said. In their haste, no one had remembered to call the police.

"Yes, I'll do that now." replied Ruby, another waitress, reaching for the phone and dialing 911.

The police arrived and took Margaret's statement. No one else had seen the mugging, so they had no information to offer. There were no cameras in the parking lot, so there was no documented evidence of the attack. The officer looked at his notebook and shook his head. "Based on what you've told me, I don't have much to go on. You did not see his face or how he was dressed or anything. It appears it was just a crime of opportunity. Right place, right time. I would advise you to change your locks, call your credit card companies, and your cell phone carrier."

Carol hugged her friend, trying her best to console her. "Do you still have your car keys?" asked Carol. "No. They fell when he attacked me. I think they're still lying on the ground." Lou turned to two of his cooks, "Harry, Jake, go check to see if you find Margaret's car keys."

They left to do what Lou asked and returned shortly with the keys. "Margaret, you can't go home tonight. You have to stay with me, at least until your locks are changed," said Carol.

"How will I get home?" Margaret asked nervously. "I don't want to leave my car here, but I don't think I can drive." Her whole body was visibly shaking as she looked from Carol to Lou and back again.

"I'll drive," replied Carol. "I have my driver's license. I just can't afford a car."

"Yes," Lou replied. "I'll drive behind you to make sure you both get home safely."

"Thanks, Lou. Thanks, everybody." Margaret replied, looking around at her coworkers. They finished closing up the diner and then left together with Lou escorting Carol and Margaret to Carol's apartment.

Lou couldn't help being angry at himself. "I knew I should have had those extra lights and cameras installed. First thing tomorrow, I'm calling that company to come in and install them. I can't afford for anyone else to get hurt," he told himself.

58

Luke headed for a clump of bushes not far from the highway, Margaret's pocketbook clutched tightly in his hand. The first order of business was to make sure that this was indeed Margaret, the wife who had left him almost two years ago.

"I've heard of people having the same name, but what are the chances of them resembling each other? Is she one of a twin that was separated at birth? I doubt it. We grew up together, and I've never heard of her having a twin. If this is really my Margaret, then I have a lesson to teach her—one she'll never forget," Luke told himself. Still holding on to the pocketbook, he snaked his way through the bushes and headed toward a nearby street light.

He quickly looked around to make sure he was not being observed. Except for the sounds of the highway traffic in the distance, all was quiet. He dumped the contents of the pocketbook onto the ground and located a wallet. He ripped it open and removed the driver's license. He stared at the picture for a very long time.

Yes, this is my long lost wife. I hope you'll be happy to see me. I know I will be!

He smiled at the thought. He committed Margaret's address to memory and then tossed her driver's license aside. He removed all the cash, credit cards, cell phone, and last of all, the keys to Margaret's condo.

He now had all he needed to keep him comfortable until the time came for him to pay a visit to his wife. His next order of business was to find a place where he could buy some new clothes and a hotel where he could take a long hot shower and get a good night's sleep.

"I guess I'll stick around this town for a while. Something tells me I'm going to like it here," he said to himself as he headed for a nearby mall.

Margaret spent a very restless night on Carol's couch. Her dreams were filled with sinister creatures that were attempting to strangle her. More than once she woke up frightened, cold sweat washing over her body. Morning arrived, but she felt more tired that when she went to bed.

She dragged herself off the couch and headed for the kitchen. "I need coffee," she said to Carol, sitting down in the nearest chair. They had breakfast together, but Margaret did not have much of an appetite. Before leaving for work, Carol hugged Margaret.

"I wish I could stay and help you, but you know Carmen is still out on maternity leave. If I don't go in, they're going to be going crazy."

Margaret nodded understandably. "I know, I know. You go ahead, I'll be fine," she told Carol.

"Stay as long as you like," Carol told her. "When I get off work, I'll go back to your condo with you."

"Thanks, Carol," replied Margaret. "But I need to get a locksmith to change the locks, plus I need to make some calls. I'll be fine."

"Okay, just be careful," Carol warned her. "Call me if you need anything, or if you just need to talk." Carol rushed off, leaving Margaret alone to sort out the confusion that was now her life.

Margaret went back to bed, hoping she would make up the sleep she had lost, but that was just not happening. After tossing and turning, she decided not to waste the entire day but to try and get some work done. Time had flown by, and it was now almost twelve o'clock.

"I can't believe the day is going by so fast," she said to herself.

Using Carol's home phone, the first call she placed was to a locksmith who promised to meet her at her condo within the hour.

"That was easy," she said to herself. "I hope my other calls go as well."

The next call was to the bank where she had her credit card account. She connected with the customer service department and verified that she was indeed Margaret Foster. "I was mugged last night, and my credit card was stolen. I'd like to have it cancelled before the thief gets a chance to use it." She asked the customer service representative to issue a new card—but was she in for a surprise!

"Ms. Foster, your card has been maxed out. Apparently your mugger went on a spending spree. He racked up a total of five thousand dollars."

Thinking she had not heard properly, she asked, "What did you just say? I don't think I heard you."

The customer service representative repeated herself. Had she not been already sitting down, Margaret would have fainted.

"Where was the card used?" she barely managed to get the words out.

"At a local department store, a hotel, and cash advance," replied the customer service representative.

"Thank you," Margaret whispered.

The customer service representative continued talking about mailing her another card, but Margaret's attention had long been diverted. She barely remembered hanging up the phone.

Things went better with the phone company, and she was able to have a replacement phone without much trouble. She spent the remainder of the morning making several calls trying to sort things out and to reclaim her stolen life.

"I can't believe how much of our private lives we carry around on our persons. From now on, I'll have to do things differently," she vowed to herself.

59

Margaret met with the locksmith within the hour as promised, who assured her that the old lock had not been tampered with.

At least he did not get a chance to use the old keys, she thought to herself.

He installed a new lock and added an additional dead bolt lock to ensure Margaret's piece of mind. He left shortly after making sure she knew how to use them correctly.

"Thank you. I feel a bit safer now," she told him.

She called Carol to let her know that she had returned to her condo, and Carol promised to come by on her way from work. She walked from room to room, taking inventory as it were. She wanted to satisfy herself that everything was as it should be, and that no intruder had visited during the night. She felt nervous but told herself that was normal for anyone whose privacy had been so invaded. She soon had every inch of her condo covered and slowly started to relax and put the incident behind her. She brewed some tea, filled her cup, and made herself comfortable on her favorite couch. She turned on the television and told herself, "I'll watch some TV and maybe take a nap before Carol comes by." She scrolled through the TV channels, looking for a worthwhile program to watch. The doorbell sounded, interrupting her search.

"Who can that be?" she asked herself nervously. "I'm really not in the mood for company today." Thinking it was possibly someone trying to sell her something she didn't really need, she headed for the front door. "I'll get rid of whoever it is fast and get back to watching my program," she told herself.

She looked through the peephole of her front door. Standing with his back to the door was a tall, dark-haired man surveying the surroundings. He had his hands in his pocket and looked as if he was master of all he surveyed. Margaret anxiously waited for him to face the door. At last he does!

Margaret staggered backward, almost losing her balance as she looked into the handsome face of a familiar-looking stranger. Hands trembling, she wiped her face and took a shallow breath. "It can't be! He's dead. I saw him drive over that bridge with my own two eyes." Thinking she has made a mistake, she pulled herself together and sneaked another look through the peephole.

"It's Luke. It's him, all right. I'd know those blue eyes anywhere. I should have changed my name. But how did he find me?" Feeling faint, she leaned against the stair railing. The doorbell rang again, this time followed by impatient banging.

"What am I going to do?" she whispered to herself.

Trembling, she moved toward the door, still deciding whether to open it or not. However, that decision is now taken out of her hands as with a loud bang, the door crashed in.

"Hello, Meg. Don't I get a welcome kiss?" he asked sweetly as he strode toward Margaret, arms extended.

Eyes wide with fear, Margaret swallowed hard as his long legs brought him closer and closer. It was as if time moved in slow motion as all the evil she had endured with him started coming back to her. Eyes closed tightly, she prayed quietly, "Oh God, please let this be a dream." She was unsure if she said the words out loud or if they were only in her mind.

Stranger At The Door

Margaret backed away from the door with her eyes closed, wishing she could make herself invisible. Luke kept advancing toward her, fists tightly clenched. She opened her eyes just in time to see him reaching for her throat. The welcoming smile had disappeared, and in its place was the familiar sneer that Margaret knew so well. She ducked and ran. *If I go upstairs, I'll be trapped*, she thought. The closest place that offered some degree of safety was the laundry room. *If I could just make it in and lock the door, I'll be okay for a while*, she thought.

As she ran, she was reliving her escape from Plains all over again. Her feet grew wings as she flew down the corridor with Luke right on her heels. She barely made it into the small laundry room, slammed the door, and threw the lock. *Now to get some weight behind the door*, she thought. Summoning all her strength, she pushed and shoved until she had the washing machine wedged behind the door. Luke jiggled the door handle, but it refused to budge.

"Open the door, Margaret!" he yelled. She made no reply. She could hear him kicking at the door over and over again. It was an interior door, hollow and not as strong as an outer door, and she knew it wouldn't withstand an attack for much longer. She leaned against the washer, breathing hard, hoping help would arrive soon.

She knew fear—it was nothing new—and this was it. As familiar as she was with fear, she thought she had seen the last of it when she escaped from Plains. Suddenly all became quiet in the corridor. Margaret knew that Luke did not give up easily, and he was patiently waiting and planning his next move.

Ventilation was not the best in the small laundry room, and soon she started feeling the effects of the confined space. Suddenly there was a loud banging on the door—more like a chopping sound. She listened again, trying to determine what was going on. She didn't have long to wait. She suddenly jumped at the sound of splintering wood. *Lord, help me. He is chopping down the door!* Margaret panicked.

She backed away from the door, fearing she would be injured from the flying splinters. The chopping sound continued, and with each blow, Luke vented his anger. It was as if he were chopping Margaret into tiny pieces.

"How dare you run away from me…" *Whump.*

"I have searched long and hard for you…" *Whump.*

"And I am not going to let you get away again…" *Whump.*

Finally, the door gave way and crashed in. The washing machine was the only thing that separated Margaret from the crazy man now standing before her. Luke angrily pushed aside the washer as if it were a feather. There was now nothing standing in the way of him getting to her.

60

Margaret stood her ground. She had made her decision. She was tired of running. In her heart she had decided, *If today is the day for me to die, then so be it. I'd rather die than let him see the fear that I feel.* With her heart almost beating out of her chest, she stood her ground and looked him in the eye, unafraid.

"Okay, so here you are. What's your next move?" she asked. She had no idea where this sudden bravado was coming from but was determined to go with it.

Luke stepped into the room, perspiration washing over his face, his shirt soaked from the strenuous work with the ax. He grabbed Margaret by the throat, hate flowing through every fiber of those piercing blue eyes. "I'll show you what's next," he spat out.

He lifted the ax over his head, preparing to rain down blows on Margaret's head. Suddenly a blow connected with the back of his head, knocking him off his feet. The ax fell from his hand, and his knees buckled as he grabbed onto the back of his head. He saw stars as he angrily turned to see who had landed the blow. His vision was blurred, but not to the point where he could not recognize a vaguely familiar face. Roaring like an injured animal, he staggered to his feet and headed toward the corridor, looking for the person who had dared to hit him.

No longer in immediate physical danger, Margaret quickly ran from the laundry room, grabbed her phone from the kitchen counter, and started dialing 911. She might be ready to die, but it would be foolish to go without reaching out for help when it was a phone call away.

Luke staggered into the kitchen. Suddenly he was face to face with a female holding a skillet. He stopped, wondering where he had seen her before. It suddenly came back to him. Luke shot her a withering look. "Well…so not only can you serve a decent meal, but you can also deliver a killer blow as well."

Still holding on to the skillet, Carol stared him down. She started taunting him. "Come on, big man. Show me what you've got. You like hitting on women, come on, hit me. I dare you…"

Luke grabbed for the skillet but was still too unsteady on his feet to make a connection. Carol kept up the taunting, eluding him time after time. Gradually the pain in his head subsided, his vision returned, and his gait got steadier.

Sitting on the kitchen counter was a butcher block holding a number of knives. Luke grabbed for the closest one, which happened to be a large chopping knife with serrated edges. He lunged at Carol but missed as she quickly sidestepped him. Margaret stood quietly by, waiting for a chance to sneak by Luke while he was still occupied with Carol. An opportunity soon presented itself, and she made a dash for the front door. However, Luke was faster! He caught and held Margaret in a headlock with the knife at her throat. Margaret fought for her life as she had never fought before.

"Stop struggling. Do you know how long and hard I've searched for you? I'm not about to let you get away now," he rambled. Margaret kept fighting, but the harder she struggled, the tighter Luke held on. Soon she was finding it harder and harder to breathe. Carol watched as Margaret struggled without success. She could not stand by and let her friend continue to suffer. Wiping away her tears, she went after Luke again, hitting him with the skillet wherever she saw an opening, but none of her blows were having any effect.

Luckily, Margaret's call had gone through. Although she was not able to talk to a 911 operator, the phone line was open, and they were able to track the address. Soon the sound of sirens was heard drawing closer and closer, but Luke was oblivious to the sound. His main focus was on taking the life of the woman who had caused him so much pain. As his hold on Margaret's neck tightened, she started losing consciousness. Luke was now like a mad man, his eyes as wild as a wounded animal.

"Now I got you. Try and run if you can," he snarled, looking at Margaret with all the hatred he could muster. Margaret could not respond. The blood supply carrying lifesaving oxygen to her brain had been drastically interrupted. With his arm still around her neck, he roughly dragged her back to the laundry room. As her feet trailed on the floor, small pieces of wood splinters became lodged in her bare feet. A thin trail of blood followed her into the laundry room, marring the beauty of what was once her beautiful travertine floor. He released his hold on her, and she slumped to the floor, unmoving.

Once he entered the room, he tried creating a barrier between him and the police. After all, who knew how long he might have to remain there! He proceeded to replace both the washer and dryer to where the door once stood, creating a makeshift barrier. It was far from sturdy, and he knew it. However, he told himself, "This will have to do."

Additional police cars pulled up in front of the condo, and a number of officers quickly alighted. Carol hurried to the door to meet them. Barely able to speak through her tears, she pointed to the door where Luke was holding Margaret hostage. "They're in the laundry room…He has a knife to her throat," she said as she continued crying.

"What's his name?" one officer asked.

"Luke Foster," Carol replied. The officers looked at each other knowingly. They were all dressed in their bulletproof vests, ready to contain the situation, maintain a perimeter, and move all the curious gawkers out of the immediate area. The first officer cautiously entered the condo, hands hovering near his gun. He slowly worked his way toward the laundry room and called out.

"Mr. Foster, I'm Officer Hall. Why don't you let your wife go so we can talk?"

"I'm in no mood to talk today," Luke called back. The officer continued moving toward the laundry room, all senses on alert. "Don't come any closer, or I'll cut her throat," Luke called out.

"That wouldn't be good for anyone, Mr. Foster. Is there anything we can do for you?" the officer asked.

"No, I have all that I need right here," Luke replied. The officer was now in front of the laundry room, looking into the deranged face of Luke Foster. Margaret was lying on the ground, barely breathing, her face a pale sickly color.

The officer looked at her and then at Luke. "She looks like she's not breathing," said the officer, concern in his voice.

"Don't worry about her, she's fine," Luke warned, barely glancing down at Margaret.

"She doesn't look fine to me," the officer replied.

Luke glared at the officer, hatred all over his face. *No one seems to understand what this woman has done to me*, he thought to himself. *She made me kill a police officer, and now I'm going to have to go to jail. I might even get the death penalty. The least I can do is teach her a lesson about what happens to any woman who tries to leave me…let her feel what it's like to really hurt.*

"Make it easy on yourself, Luke. Let her go. She needs medical help," the officer said. "If she dies, things will not go easy for you."

Luke laughed. "Things will not go easy for me whichever way you look at it."

The SWAT team soon arrived and was quickly apprised of the situation. "What demands has he made?" asked the leader of the SWAT team.

"He has no demands," replied the officer. "He says he has all that he needs."

"What does that mean?" asked the SWAT leader.

"I think the only thing he wants is his wife," the officer replied with a shrug.

"Well," returned the SWAT officer. "That's not the way to go about getting her."

The SWAT team leader gathered his men around him and quickly worked out their strategy. Soon they separated, the hostage negotiator heading toward the laundry room while the others took their position in predetermined areas. Reaching the laundry room, the negotiator moved to a spot where he could make eye contact with Luke.

"Hello, Mr. Foster. I'm Officer Cargill. What can we do to bring this situation to a peaceful end?" he asked.

"Like I told the first officer, I don't need anything. I have all that I need right here," he said, looking down at Margaret.

"How about some water. It looks quite hot in there. Can I get you some water or something cool to drink?"

Luke wiped the perspiration from his face and replied. "Okay, I'd like some water."

The water soon arrived, and the negotiator moved as if to enter the room. Reaching for the knife, Luke told him, "Stop right there. You can leave it on the machine. I'll get it from there. Now back out."

The officer complied, moving a few steps back while still making eye contact. "Is there anything else I can get you, Luke? Can I call you Luke?" asked the negotiator.

"No, I don't need anything, and yes, you can call me Luke," he replied.

"Okay. Luke, there must be something that you need. I can't imagine that you plan to stay in here indefinitely. If there is anything at all that I can do for you, just let me know."

"I don't know. I need to think," Luke said angrily, combing his hands through his hair and wiping perspiration from his face.

"How about Margaret? She looks as though she needs some medical attention. If she dies, that's not going to work in your favor," the negotiator continued. Luke made no reply. The negotiator tried again. "Come on, Luke. Each minute that goes by, she could be getting worse."

"I'm still thinking," replied Luke angrily. The minutes slowly ticked by as Luke wrestled with himself. No matter what decision he made today, he knew he had come to the end of the line. He knew he was guilty of so much, and the only reason he was still a free man was because luck had been on his side. But now even that seemed to be finally running out. An hour flew by, and still Luke refused to give up. Each time the negotiator asked if he was ready to give up, he would reply that he was still thinking. It was now getting dark, and patience was starting to wear thin. The negotiator finally decided to bring things to an end. "This is your last chance, Luke," said the negotiator. "If you're not coming out, then I'm coming in."

Luke was tired both in body and spirit. He could run no longer. He had reached the end of the line, and so he made his decision. "Okay," he said to the officer, "I'm coming out. But I want to make a deal."

"Sorry, Luke, no deals. Come on out. No sudden moves or I'll have to bring you down," the negotiator warned. Luke made no comment. He started walking toward the negotiator. "Keep your hands up where I can see them," warned the negotiator. He gave a prearranged signal, and the remaining team members quietly moved toward the laundry room. Suddenly Luke reached down, scooping up Margaret along with the knife. "I'm not going without her," he said angrily. He brought Margaret's limp body up to his chest to form a protective shield. The negotiator brought his weapon in position and calmly replied, "Release her now. I will not tell you again."

Luke laughed as he fought to hold Margaret's limp body upright. The weight of her unconscious body kept sliding down; she was solid dead weight, and the effects was starting to tell on him. As he moved, her head kept lolling about on his chest, exposing his upper shoulder, chest, and arms. That was all the SWAT negotiator needed. He took aim, and a bullet found its mark into Luke's left shoulder. Margaret immediately fell from his hand onto the floor, unmoving. The knife flew from his hand as he grabbed onto his chest. Disbelief was visible all over his face. He couldn't belief he had just been shot. He opened his mouth to scream, but his voice had deserted him. He fell next to Margaret, his blood gushing all over her. However, Margaret was unaware of being drenched with the blood of the man who had intentionally drawn blood from her so many, many times. The sound of the gunshot quickly brought other officers running. The front room quickly filled with paramedics, local police officers, and firemen all making their way into the laundry room. They pushed aside the flimsy blockade, and the first group of paramedics quickly turned their attention to the bleeding convict while the other group tended to an unconscious Margaret.

Epilogue

As Luke fell to the floor, bright-red blood gushed from his wound like a newly tapped oil well. It was clear that a main artery had been hit, and if emergency measures were not immediately implemented, there would be one dead convict on their hands. But who would miss Luke Foster if he died? Certainly not Margaret; she had had as much of him as she could tolerate and so much more than she deserved. As it was, she was in desperate need of immediate medical attention herself. If anyone deserved to be spared, it was her. But the paramedics brought back to mind the words of the Hippocratic oath: "I will remember that I remain a member of society, with special obligations to all my fellow human beings…" And so they continued to give Luke their all until the straight line and the beeping of the heart monitor told them it was futile to continue with their efforts.

The second group of paramedics had turned their attention to Margaret. The paramedics applied an oxygen mask to her face, and her respirations gradually became regular and unlabored. She moaned softly as full consciousness returned. Finally, her eyes fluttered open, and she stared around blankly. Finally recognition dawned. She breathed deeply, allowing the oxygen to enter her body and flow to all the vital organs that had been temporarily deprived. As the significance of the situation dawned on her, she closed her eyes for a moment and let the tears run unchecked down her cheeks. She took another deep breath and sent up a silent prayer of gratitude. It had taken a while, but at long last her prayer had been answered. She no longer had to live in fear. Like David and Goliath, her nemesis had been eliminated.